2.75

"You've got to calm down. I'm not going to hurt you," the voice said, but his words barely penetrated Sophia's terrorized brain.

She was desperate to get his hand off her mouth. She allowed her knees to give way so all her body weight fell. He didn't let go of her face, but he did let her hands go so he could grip her weight with his other arm.

Sophia reached up and grasped the hand covering her mouth with both of her hands—her need for air overwhelming all other thoughts.

"Are you trying to get us both killed?" the voice hissed.

Now there was no doubt in Sophia's mind that the voice was familiar. She shook loose from the arm that held her and turned to face the source of the voice. When she saw him clearly she almost stumbled again.

Just as tall, dark and handsome as ever—a walking cliché. The man who had walked out of her life five years ago. Without one single word.

"Cameron?"

INFILTRATION

—

Janie Crouch

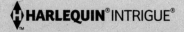

To my sweet coz, the real "Sophia." Thanks
for providing the strength, charm and beauty
to model a character after (although the rest is
sheer drama and not you, I promise).
I am thankful beyond measure to have you
in my life—a cousin by birth, a sister in
every other way. 143, FC1!

ISBN-13: 978-0-373-69811-0

Infiltration

Copyright © 2015 by Janie Crouch

Recycling programs
for this product may
not exist in your area.

Printed in U.S.A.

HARLEQUIN®
™www.Harlequin.com

Janie Crouch has loved to read romance her whole life. She cut her teeth on Harlequin Romances as a preteen, then moved on to a passion for romantic suspense as an adult.

Janie lives with her husband and four children in Virginia, where she teaches communication courses at a local college. Janie enjoys traveling, long-distance running, movie-watching, knitting and adventure/obstacle racing. You can find out more about her at janiecrouch.com.

Books by Janie Crouch

Harlequin Intrigue

Primal Instinct

Omega Sector
Infiltration

CAST OF CHARACTERS

Cameron Branson—Omega Sector agent on a deep undercover mission with crime syndicate group DS-13. Wants justice for his partner who was murdered by them, and will let nothing get in his way.

Sophia Reardon—A graphic artist for the FBI, not interested in any sort of clandestine operations. She's got enough problems of her own, just getting through day by day.

Mr. Smith—The elusive leader of DS-13, responsible for Cameron's partner's death. Cameron's ultimate goal is to meet and arrest him, but that has proved more difficult than Cameron imagined.

Fin—Member of DS-13 and Cameron's link to meeting Mr. Smith.

Rick—Another member of DS-13. Enjoys cruelty.

Fred McNeil—FBI agent on DS-13's payroll.

Dylan Branson—Cameron's strong and quiet older brother. Past operative for Omega Sector, now runs a small delivery/courier business with his own airplane.

Sawyer Branson—Cameron's charming younger brother. Current agent Omega Sector.

Dennis Burgamy—Cameron's boss at Omega Sector.

Chapter One

Cameron Branson had been telling the lies so long he was afraid they were becoming truth to him.

"Look, Tom, I don't have a lot of time," Cameron barked quietly into his cell phone as he sat on a bench and looked out at Washington, DC's Potomac River. Joggers ran by in front of him and a mother chased a squealing toddler, but Cameron paid them no mind.

He especially paid no attention to the man sitting on the other side of the bench next to him who was also on his cell phone while glancing at a newspaper.

Except neither man was actually talking on his cell phone. They were talking to each other.

"Protocol dictates that we meet twice a week unless circumstances prove it impossible," Cameron was reminded by "Tom."

"Yeah, well, I don't have a whole lot of concern about protocol right at this moment. What I care about is bringing down the SOB who killed Jason."

Tom sighed and turned the page on his newspaper, without ever looking at Cameron. "You've been under a long time, Cam. And you missed our last two scheduled meetings. I can only cover for you so much before higher-ups start noticing."

"Well, it's not always easy getting away from the bad

guys so we can have our chats," Cameron all but sneered. He knew his anger at Tom was misplaced, but couldn't seem to keep his irritation under control. He just wanted to get back to work.

"Everybody knows your undercover work in DS-13 is critical for us and for you personally. But it's important for us to do things by the book."

Cameron sighed but didn't say what was on his mind: doing things by the book was probably what had gotten Cameron's previous partner killed.

"All right. I'm sorry. I'll try to do better." Cameron almost believed it as he said it.

"Is everything still on for tomorrow's buy?"

"Yeah. It should go without a hiccup. Just make sure the warehouse stays clear."

"Cameron, I needed to meet with you about something else." Tom closed his newspaper and then reopened it. He seemed to be hesitating. Cameron knew this was bad. He'd never known his handler to be at a loss for words. "The parameters of your mission have changed."

Damn. "How so?"

"Taking the members and leader of DS-13 into custody is no longer your primary objective. For neither their black market activities nor their presumed part in your partner's death."

"Dammit, Tom..."

"I know, Cameron. But recent intel notified us that DS-13 has obtained new encoding-transmitting technologies that they'll be selling to terrorists."

Cameron sighed and waited for Tom to continue.

"It's called Ghost Shell. This technology is like nothing we've ever seen—it could cripple communication within government agencies. It would give multiple terrorist groups the edge they've been looking for, and open us up to attacks all over the country. It's critical that this technology doesn't make it to the black market."

"Why isn't the cyberterrorism unit on this?" Cameron murmured with a sigh.

"It's beyond cyberterrorism now. Straight into terrorism. Besides, it's already out in the open. And since you're already neck-deep in DS-13…"

Cameron just shook his head. He knew what Tom said was true. Technology like this in DS-13's hands—the group was solely focused on financial gain—was bad, but in the hands of terrorist groups who were intent on destruction and loss of life, it would mean disaster.

"Roger that, Tom. Change of primary objective confirmed. I'll be in touch when I know something." Cameron got up from the bench and walked away. Tom stayed, as Cameron knew he would, pretending to talk on his cell phone a while longer as he looked at the paper.

Yeah, Cameron's primary objective had changed. But he'd be damned if he'd let justice for his partner's memory suffer because of it.

THE NEXT DAY, sitting in the back of the extended SUV with windows tinted just a bit darker than what was probably legal, Cam Cameron, as he was known to DS-13, pretended to chuckle at a filthy joke told by one of the other riders. When a second rider chimed in with another joke—something about a blonde, a redhead and a brunette—Cameron just tuned them out. He stretched his long legs out in front of him. At least there was room to do that in this vehicle.

One thing he had to give DS-13: they may be an organized crime ring with ties to almost every criminal activity imaginable—weapons, drugs, human trafficking, to name a few—but they knew how to travel in style.

Cameron had been undercover with them for eight months. Eight months pretending to be a midlevel weapons dealer. Eight months of trying to move up in the ranks of DS-13, so he could meet the boss.

The man who had ordered the execution of Cameron's partner over a year ago.

Cameron had made very little progress in the meeting-the-boss area of his work. Instead he'd been stuck with lower-level minions, who evidently thought a punch line about high heels and a sugar daddy downright hilarious, given the guffawing coming from all corners of the vehicle. Cameron chuckled again, just so it wouldn't be obvious that he wasn't laughing.

Blending in was key. Cameron's looks—black hair just a little too long, dark brown eyes, a perpetual five o'clock shadow—made him particularly suited for blending in with bad guys. Cameron had specifically cultivated the dark and unapproachable look. His six-foot frame was muscular—made even more so over the past few months since a favorite activity of the DS-13 minions was lifting weights—and he was light on his feet.

All in all, Cameron knew he came across as someone not to be messed with. Someone who could take care of himself. Someone menacing. It had helped him in undercover work for years, this ability to blend in physically.

The problem was, he felt his soul starting to blend in, too.

"Cam, don't you know any good jokes, man?" the driver called back to Cameron.

The best joke I know will be on you guys when I arrest all you bastards.

"No, Fin. I don't know any jokes. I can't be this beautiful, able to outlift all you princesses *and* be able to tell jokes. Wouldn't be fair to the rest of the world." Cameron smirked.

This led to an immediate argument over which of the four people in the SUV could bench the most weight, as Cameron knew it would.

Cameron was tired. He was tired of the lies, tired of keeping one step ahead of everyone else, tired of spending every day with these morons. And yesterday's meeting with Tom had confirmed what Cameron had already known: he wasn't checking in with his handler at Omega Sector as often as he should.

But since Cameron worked for Omega—an elite interagency task force—there was a little more leeway about check-ins and staying undercover longer. Omega agents had more training, more experience and the distinct mental acuity needed for long-term undercover work, or they never were sent out in the first place.

They were the best of the best.

God, it sounded so *Top Gun*. And Cameron certainly didn't feel best of anything right now.

"Two-ninety clean and jerk, two-seventy bench," Cameron responded to one of the guys asking about his top weight-lifting ability.

A round of obscenities flew through the vehicle. Nobody believed him.

"I'll take any of you pansies on, at any time." Cameron looked down at his fingernails in boredom. "But you better call your mommies first."

Another round of obscenities about what they would do to his mother, then arguments resumed about lifting, leg weights this time. Cameron zoned out again.

Cameron had promised Tom he would check in with the handler more often. He wasn't particularly worried about what Tom or the agency would do if he didn't. But he was worried his brothers, one older, one younger, both with ties to Omega Sector, might decide to storm the castle if they thought Cameron was in trouble. Not to mention his sister.

He wasn't in trouble, at least not the type that required help from his siblings.

He knew he was starting to make some progress in the case; there were talks of taking Cameron to the DS-13 main base, wherever that was. That's what Cameron wanted. That's where he would meet the man who ordered his partner's death. And as soon as Cameron could link him with that or any other felony, that bastard was going down.

Oh, yeah, and Cameron would recover Ghost Shell, as ordered.

Cameron didn't take the orders about the technology acquirement lightly. He would get it. But he would bring down the bad guys while he was at it.

And then Cameron could get out of undercover work for a while and try to find himself. Get away from lies and filth for an extended period. Try to remember why he started this job in the first place.

As the SUV pulled up to an abandoned warehouse in a suburb far outside of Washington, Cameron got his head back in the game. No point whining about how hard this job was; he'd known that for a while now. Five years to be exact. Cameron immediately pushed that thought out of his head. This wasn't the time or place to think about her. Or any of the disasters that had happened since.

Opening his car door, Cameron stepped out. "All right, ladies, everything should be in the back office, upstairs. Use the east entrance since it's least visible."

The driver, Fin, was the leader of the group. Cameron walked around the car to him. "How do you want to set up security, Fin?" Cameron knew it was important to make Fin feel as if he was in charge.

"Yeah, let's leave someone at the back door outside and someone walking around inside, just in case."

Cameron nodded. "Great." He knew there would be no raids by authorities or attacks by a rival organization—thanks to Omega Sector—but nobody else knew it. As a matter of fact, nobody but them should be around this area at all. "You're coming in with me, right? So we can get it all counted and tested?"

Cameron was the one who had set up this sale, in an attempt to prove his usefulness, again, to DS-13. The men inside the warehouse—bad guys in their own right—were business associates of Cameron's. They were going to buy the weapons, ones Cameron had gotten for DS-13 at a hugely reduced price, thanks to them actually coming from the Omega Sector armory. All in all, DS-13 would make a nice little profit for very little work. Cameron would come out looking like the golden boy and would hopefully be one step closer to meeting the man in charge.

Nobody in DS-13 would ever know that the scumbags buying the weapons would be picked up by local law enforcement a few miles down the road after leaving here. The weapons would go back into government lockdown.

Fin barked orders to the rest of the men then walked with Cameron up the outdoor stairs to the second floor of the building. Inside was an office that looked down on the expanse of the warehouse, except seeing through the windows was nearly impossible due to years of cleaning neglect.

Cameron introduced the buyers to Fin and then stepped aside to let Fin talk to them so the guy could feel as if he was in charge. Cameron walked over to stand by a window that looked out onto the road. He rubbed a tiny bit of the filthy pane with his finger so he could see out, all the while keeping his ear on the conversation between the buyers and Fin, making sure Fin didn't screw things up.

Looking out his tiny hole, Cameron noticed a car moving slowly from the warehouse next door toward them. He cursed silently. Nobody was supposed to be in this area at all except for them. Omega Sector should've seen to that.

When the car got out of his line of sight from that window, Cameron casually moved to another window. He leaned back against the wall for a few moments before turning nonchalantly to the window and once again creating a little peephole in the dirt. Cameron was careful not to make it look as if he was studying anything. The last thing he wanted to do was draw attention to that car.

Sure enough the vehicle stopped right in front of the warehouse. Cameron cursed under his breath again. He hoped Marco, the man Fin had left as guard, didn't see the car. Maybe he wouldn't. The minions tended to be a little slack when Fin wasn't watching. Marco may be out smoking by the SUV or something. Cameron desperately hoped so. The last thing he needed was some civilian caught up in this mess.

"Isn't that right, Cam?" Fin called out to Cameron.

Cameron racked his brain trying to figure out what they were talking about. He needed to be paying more attention to this sale. Cameron wasn't sure how to respond. He didn't want to let on that he hadn't been listening to the conversation when he was the one who had set the whole thing up in the first place. Cameron decided to take a chance.

"If you say it, then it must be true, Fin."

Both the buyers and Fin burst out laughing, so Cameron figured he had said the right thing. He watched as Fin began showing the weapons to the buyers.

When he turned to the window again, the driver had gotten out of the car. He couldn't see much, but it looked as if it was a lone woman.

Damn.

Cameron knew he had to get down there and try to divert disaster before it hit full force.

"Fin, I've got to take a leak. I'm sure there's a can downstairs somewhere. I'll be back in a sec."

Fin and the buyers barely looked up from their exchange. Fin shooed in Cameron's general direction with his hand. Normally this lack of regard would've irritated Cameron, but now he was thankful for it. He headed out the door leading into the main section of the warehouse.

He hoped whoever was in the car was just some poor idiot who had gotten lost and would soon be on her way.

SOPHIA REARDON WAS lost and felt like some poor idiot. She rolled her window down farther and took a few deep breaths of air, trying to refocus.

Was this warehouse really the place? All of them looked the same. If she could read her own handwriting that would help. Of course, if people would do their jobs correctly in the first place she wouldn't have to be here at the corner of Serial-Killers-R-Us Street and Shouldn't-Be-Here-Alone Avenue.

Sophia looked down at the napkin where she'd scribbled the address. Yeah, that was definitely an *8* not a *3*. Which meant it was *this* warehouse she was supposed to be at, not the just-as-scary first one she'd gone to.

All Sophia needed were a few pictures of the interior ceiling frame and doorway of the warehouse to help finish a computer rendering of the building. This warehouse was identical to one that had burned down in an arson case two weeks ago—the work of a serial arsonist who had hit buildings in four different states. The FBI had been called in to help local law enforcement.

Sophia muttered under her breath again as she grabbed her camera gear and purse. She put her FBI credentials in her pocket, in case some poor security guard needed to see them. She pushed open the door to the warehouse and walked in slowly, giving her eyes time to adjust. She cursed her office mate, Bruce, who had begged Sophia to take these pictures.

"'The new girl at the coffee shop said yes to lunch, Sophia,'" Sophia said in her best mimicry of Bruce's voice. "'But today's our only chance this week. Please, please, please go take pictures at the horror-film warehouse for me. I'm worth getting mutilated for.'"

Sophia sighed. Bruce owed her. Big-time. Sophia hated this cloak-and-dagger stuff.

Sure, she worked for the FBI, but would be the first to tell you she wasn't an agent. She didn't even do CSI stuff usually, although she was part of the forensic team. She was a graphic designer, for goodness' sake. She designed brochures and fliers and posters. Safe in the comfort of her office in DC, not in some warehouse in Scaryville.

As the door closed behind her, Sophia took a deep breath and reminded herself there was plenty of air in this building and nothing to be afraid of. She was not trapped back in that car like during the accident five years ago. Sophia went through a couple of the mental exercises Dr. Fretwell had taught her to get her brief moment of panic under control. Once it had passed she grabbed her camera and began getting the shots she needed.

The doorway posed no problems so she got those first. But the beams in the ceiling area were going to be more difficult to film. Looking around she realized the office in the back would give her much better access to the shots she needed of the ceiling framing.

Sophia cautiously made her way back to the steps leading up to the office. It didn't look as if there were any serial killers or cyborgs living here, but the place still gave her the creeps. Wooden crates and boxes were piled all along the stairs and landing, making getting up them precarious. Sophia kept a firm grip on the railing for as long as she could until she had to let go to step around a huge crate.

As she began climbing the second set of steps, Sophia caught something moving out of the corner of her eye. She turned to see what it was just as an arm reached out from behind her and covered her mouth, pulling her up against a hard chest and silencing her startled scream.

A deep voice breathed quietly in her ear, "What the hell are you doing here?"

Chapter Two

Sophia was shocked into complete stillness for a moment then burst into a flurry of action. She elbowed the abs behind her and swung her legs backward at his shins. Although she heard a couple of grunts, the hand over her mouth didn't move.

Terror completely overwhelmed her. The hand was cutting off her air and she couldn't breathe. Panic made her blows even more frantic and she heard more grunts, but he still didn't release her. She reached back and tried to scratch his face, but he caught both her wrists with his free hand before she could do any damage. He pulled her closer to his chest so her kicks couldn't do any harm, either.

"You've got to calm down. I'm not going to hurt you," the voice said, but his words barely penetrated Sophia's terrorized brain.

She was desperate to get his hand off her mouth. She allowed her knees to give way so all her body weight fell. He didn't let go of her face, but he did let her hands go so he could grip her weight with his other arm.

Sophia reached up and grasped the hand covering her mouth with both of her hands, her need for air overwhelming all other thoughts. Somewhere in the back of her mind she could hear Dr. Fretwell reminding her that there was plenty of oxygen, that there was always plenty of oxygen, but she couldn't make herself believe it.

"Listen, I don't want to hurt you," the voice said again in little more than a whisper in her ear. "But I need you to calm down."

Sophia didn't believe his assurances for her safety for a second, but her only thought was to get the hand from around her mouth. It took all of her mental energy, but she forced herself to stop struggling.

"Good." The hand over her mouth eased just the slightest bit. "I'm going to let you go, but if you scream we're going to be right back in this position. Got it?"

Sophia nodded. The hand moved very slowly from her mouth, as if he was gauging whether she would keep her word not to scream. It hovered there, ready to reclamp over her mouth at the slightest noise from her. Sophia gulped air and struggled to get a hold of herself.

She wasn't going to scream. She knew there wasn't anybody around the warehouse close enough to hear it. Plus, she definitely didn't want that hand—or worse, a gag—over her mouth, cutting off her supply of oxygen. Well, not cutting off the actual supply of oxygen, but making her brain think she wasn't getting enough oxygen.

Damn claustrophobia. The last thing she needed was to become a sobbing nutcase on the floor because some creep gagged her. She needed to keep her wits about her and figure out how to get away from the big chest still standing right behind her.

Whatever trouble she was in here, she was going to have to get herself out. Because screaming wasn't going to help.

"Are you okay?" the voice asked, the mystery man still standing directly behind her, hand still hovering near her mouth.

"Yes. Look, I was just here to take some pictures of the

door and ceiling." She was breathing so hard she could barely get the words out, so Sophia lifted her camera to the side so he could see it. "Whatever you're doing here, I don't know anything about it and I don't care."

There was no response from the man behind her. Sophia didn't know if that was a good or bad thing.

"I haven't seen you. I have no idea what you look like. I'll just leave. There's no cell phone coverage out here, so it's not like I can call anyone or anything." Sophia didn't know if that was true or not. She had forgotten to charge her phone again last night, so it was sitting dead out in her car. But she wasn't about to tell him that.

She realized she was rambling, but the longer he was silent, the more she was afraid he was going to do something terrible to her, like kill her.

Or cover her mouth with his hand again.

"I'm just going to go, okay?" Sophia took a small step away from him. "I'm not going to look at you and I'm just going to go."

The arm in front of her dropped. When he didn't stop her, Sophia took another step. Then another.

"Just get in your car and leave immediately. Don't let anybody else see you or believe me, the trouble will be much worse."

Now that the voice wasn't whispering, it sounded vaguely familiar. As Sophia took another step away she turned to look at the man behind her before she could stop herself.

But before she could get a good look at him she tripped over one of the boxes lining the stairs. She grasped for the railing but couldn't reach it.

Just as she began to plummet down the stairs an arm reached out and grabbed her around her hips, sweeping her easily off her feet and yanking her back against him.

"Are you trying to get us both killed?" the voice hissed.

Now there was no doubt in Sophia's mind that the voice was familiar. She shook loose from the arm that held her and turned to face the voice. When she saw him clearly she almost stumbled again.

Just as tall, dark and handsome as ever—a walking cliché. The man who had walked out of her life five years ago. Without one single word.

"Cameron?"

Sophia watched as shock stole over Cameron's face. He was obviously as surprised to see her as she was to see him.

"Sophia? What are you doing here?"

"I'm taking pictures for a friend, for an arson investigation."

"An arson investigation? Are you law enforcement?"

Sophia shook her head. "No. Not really. I mean kind of, but no."

Cameron stared back at her in confusion and Sophia realized she wasn't making any sense.

"I work for the FBI, but I'm not an agent. I'm a graphic artist."

"You work for the Bureau? You're here for them?"

Cameron seemed overly shocked at her mention of the FBI. Sophia shook her head again. "Well, yes and no. I wasn't supposed to be here at all, but I'm helping a friend out by getting some pictures he wasn't able to get."

"Is anybody else from the Bureau coming?"

Sophia didn't understand why Cameron was asking her this, but the only thing she could think of—the only thing that really made sense about any of his behavior here—was that he was some sort of criminal now and she had walked in on something illegal.

Sophia would never have thought Cameron Branson capable of a criminal lifestyle when she had known him before. He'd just gotten out of the military and had more of a love for his family than anyone she'd ever known. He definitely had not been any sort of delinquent then. Trying to figure out where he belonged, sure. But not a criminal.

But she guessed a lot of stuff could happen in five years that changed a person. Case in point, the man standing in front of her whom she both recognized and didn't recognize.

Sophia took a step back from him. His hand, which had still been at her waist, dropped to his side.

"No, I'm not officially here for the Bureau. Nobody else is coming," Sophia told him.

Cameron seemed to relax a little at that admission, which just confirmed Sophia's suspicion about his criminal activities. Who else relaxed at the thought of the FBI *not* coming?

Sophia looked more closely at Cameron. His hair was much longer than the nearly crew-cut length he used to keep—it curled now at the top of his black T-shirt. His posture was less erect, more casual. His eyes…

Well, his eyes were still the most gorgeous shade of brown she had ever seen.

She'd nearly fallen in love with those eyes once, back when she was too young and stupid to know better. Back when she thought he was a stand-up guy who was interested in her and perhaps wanted a future together.

But she had grown up and left those dreams behind. He hadn't given her much choice, when he'd left without a goodbye and without a single word in the five years since.

So whoever this man standing in front of her was— despite his gorgeous eyes—she needed to get away from him.

For more reasons than one.

CAMERON FELT AS IF he was having an out-of-body experience as the tiny brunette who had been clawing at his face moments before transformed from a stranger into Sophia Reardon.

This was not possible.

Seriously? Of all the warehouses in all the world, she had to be in this one? And moreover, somebody from Omega should've had the roads leading down to this area blocked so nobody who wasn't supposed to be here—for example, a cute brunette with a camera—got through. Somebody was going to catch a load of trouble for this, Cameron would make sure.

But right now he had to get Sophia out of here before somebody from DS-13 saw her.

But man, she looked good. Cameron gave himself just a second to really look at her. He hadn't seen her in five years. She'd been twenty-two years old then, but she didn't seem to have changed much. Her straight brown hair was a little longer, now past her shoulders, but the natural blond highlights were still there. Through the dimness of the warehouse's lights he could barely make out the freckles that still scattered across her cheeks and nose. And her stunning green eyes.

Eyes that were glaring up at him right now. He took a step toward her but she backed up. "I'm not going to hurt you, Soph."

She stopped moving. "I know. I just… I'm pretty claustrophobic. I don't want you to cover my mouth again."

Cameron nodded. "Okay, no problem."

"Why are *you* here, Cameron?" she asked with a great deal of suspicion in her tone.

Cameron couldn't blame her for the unease, given the current situation. "It's a long story and I don't have time to explain."

She jerked away from him. "Yeah. Explanations aren't your strong suit. I remember."

Cameron winced. He reached for her again, but then let his hand fall to the side. Sophia had every right to be angry at him about how things had ended between them five years ago, even though he had never meant to hurt her. Cutting casual ties had just been part of the life he'd chosen when he took the job with Omega Sector.

Of course, the fact that he had thought about her every day since he'd walked away from her had proven to Cameron that Sophia had been more than a casual tie. Now, with quite a bit more perspective, he realized he should've given her more information and a proper goodbye.

Unfortunately, it looked as if he was about to make the same mistakes all over again: no information and no proper goodbye.

"I'm sorry, Sophia. But you have to leave. Quickly."

"And what? You'll explain later? We both know that's not true."

Cameron knew there was no real response he could give. They both did know it was true.

"Besides, I'm not sure I want to know," Sophia continued softly.

Cameron wished he could explain, at least about what was happening right now—about being undercover—but time was running out. He needed to get Sophia out of here immediately. Every moment she stayed there was more of a risk of her being seen by a member of DS-13.

"Sophia…"

She shook her head and continued before he could say anything further, reaching a hand out toward him. "Don't worry, I'm going. Whatever you're doing here, Cameron, I don't want to know. But you be careful." She drew her hand back to her side without actually touching him.

Cameron couldn't stand the look in her eyes. She thought he was a criminal. He wished he could explain. Before she could turn away, Cameron leaned down and put his forehead against hers. "I'm sorry, Soph. Again." Cameron stepped back from her. "Go as fast and as quietly as you can. Don't let anyone see you."

Cameron watched as Sophia turned and carefully manipulated her way down the stairs through all the boxes. He didn't stay to watch her go the rest of the way out. He turned and made his way back to the office.

"Get lost?" Fin snickered as Cameron walked back in.

Cam just snorted. Fin looked at him a little closer. "What happened to you? You look like you've been in a wrestling match."

Damn it. He had practically been in a wrestling match.

"Stupid boxes everywhere. It's like an obstacle course down there. I tripped." Cameron brushed his hair back into place.

That got a few chuckles. Nobody seemed suspicious, which was good. "How's it going here?" Cameron asked.

Fin was taking his time showing off to the buyers what he knew about the assault rifles being sold. Fin liked to show off whenever he knew anything about anything, and oftentimes even when he didn't, but Cameron just let him ramble on. If the buyers didn't know when and if Fin was full of crap then it was their own fault. They'd be sitting in a jail cell in a few hours anyway.

"Why don't you start counting the money, Cam?" Fin told him. Cameron barely bit back a groan of frustration. What he really wanted to do was get over to the window and make sure Sophia's car was gone. But the money was on the other side of the office.

"Sure." Cameron met one of the buyers over at the desk and pulled out a small cash-counting machine from the bag they'd brought. The machine would make things a lot faster, but not fast enough. He wanted to know—needed to know—that Sophia had made it safely out of the building. He fed the cash into the machine as quickly as he could without making it obvious that he was in a hurry. The second buyer watched him carefully the entire time.

After double-checking, because he knew Fin would ask, Cameron put the counter away.

"All here, Fin."

"Did you double-check?"

Cameron refrained from rolling his eyes. "Yes." He walked over and placed the bag of money on the table by Fin, then strolled as casually as possible over to the window.

No car. *Thank God.*

Cameron felt himself relax for the first time since he realized that the tiny brunette who had just been trying to fight her way out of his arms was Sophia. The thought of sweet Sophia being caught in the middle of this made Cameron a little sick to his stomach.

Maybe seeing her today was some sort of sign to him. Further proof he needed to finish up this case and take a break. Maybe he would call Sophia, try to repair the damage from five years ago. Explain to her his reasons for leaving.

And tell her that he had never stopped thinking about her.

But right now he had to concentrate on the case at hand. Fin was finally winding down his spiel about the assault rifles, quite a bit of it incorrect information, the buyers had the weapons they wanted and DS-13 had the cash.

Cameron could tell Fin was pleased. As the buyers left, he walked over to Cameron and slapped him on his back.

"Good job, man. Very smooth transaction."

"As always, Fin. That's what I do."

Cameron wanted to demand to meet Fin's boss, but knew that any request on his part to meet the man would push him that much further away from a meeting. He had been patient up until now. He could be patient awhile longer. Although with the Ghost Shell encoding technology becoming Cameron's prime mission objective, he couldn't be patient much longer.

Fin nodded. "It is what you do, Cam. And Mr. Smith, my…um…boss, has become well aware of that."

Cameron straightened, his interest piqued. He doubted Mr. Smith was the boss's real name, but this was the first time Fin had ever openly talked about him directly to Cameron. Finally, the slightest progress.

"Well, I'd like to meet Mr. Smith someday."

Fin slapped him on the back again. "And you will, buddy. Soon, in fact. Mr. Smith may need your help in setting up some meetings for some new stuff."

Cameron hoped that by *new stuff* Fin meant the Ghost Shell technology. Fin didn't have an expansive vocabulary, unless it came to dirty jokes.

"But now, let's get back to the house so we can see that weight lifting you were talking so much trash about on the way here."

Cameron followed Fin down the stairs. Two of the other three minions were already at the car. The third, Marco—the one sent to patrol the inside of the warehouse—wasn't there.

Dread pooled in Cameron's stomach.

"Where the hell is Marco?" Fin demanded of the other two. Neither knew.

"He's probably in there smoking or on the can. I'll go find him," Cameron offered. He had a bad feeling.

"Fine." Fin shooed Cameron annoyingly with his hand again. But again Cameron didn't care. "Hurry up."

Cameron made it to the warehouse door, just as it opened. Through it came Marco, dragging a terrified Sophia behind him.

Chapter Three

Cameron knew he had to think fast. A single word from Sophia, any sort of gesture that she knew him, would mean both their lives. In a split second, Cameron made a decision.

But he knew it wasn't going to be pretty.

He stormed up to Marco and grabbed Sophia out of his grasp. "What the hell, Marco? Is this a cop?"

Cameron pushed Sophia, probably a little rougher than necessary, face-first up against the warehouse wall. He heard her indrawn breath, but steeled himself against any thought of her pain or fear.

It was going to get much worse.

Cameron kept his hand pressed against Sophia's back, keeping her forced against the wall. Behind him he heard Fin and the other guys draw their weapons.

He willed Sophia to keep quiet.

Marco, a little shocked by Cameron's aggressive behavior, stuttered, "I just found her inside. She said she was an artist and was taking pictures of the warehouse."

"Did you check to see if she was wearing a wire or anything?" Cameron demanded.

Marco looked sheepish and shook his head. Cameron made a big show of running his hands all over Sophia's body, as if looking for surveillance equipment. Behind him the guys made a couple of catcalls. Sophia shuddered.

When his body search led to her hands, he could feel Sophia press some sort of card into his palm—he wasn't sure what. He moved so he more clearly blocked her from Fin and the men's view, and palmed whatever she had given him without looking at it. As he turned, he slipped it into the pocket of his jeans.

"She's clean," Cameron said as he spun her around. Sophia attempted to straighten the clothes Cameron had lifted and moved during his search, her face burning.

"Listen…" Sophia began.

Cameron backhanded her.

Oh, God. He pulled the slap as much as he could without making it obvious, but he knew it still had to hurt. Her head flew to the side. He watched as a bit of blood began to ooze from a split in her lip. Cameron thought he might vomit.

But if she had said his name, they would both be dead, or at the very least his undercover work would be blown. He couldn't take the chance.

He stuck his finger in her face. "You shut the hell up unless I ask you a specific question, got it?"

Cameron prayed as he had never prayed before that Sophia would keep quiet. He felt a bit of relief when she nodded slowly, staring at the ground.

"Whoa, Cam. I didn't think you had that in you." Fin chuckled.

Cameron smiled a little bit and rolled his shoulders as if he was getting rid of tension. "Yeah. Well, I hate cops. But it doesn't look like she is one."

Cameron took Sophia's digital camera and brought it over to Fin. Together they looked through the pictures. Cameron relaxed a little when they were all shots of the doorway of the warehouse.

"What are you, a photographer?" Cameron asked her. He hoped she wouldn't bring up the Bureau.

"Yeah. A graphic artist." The answer came out as little more than a whisper from Sophia. She was still looking at the ground.

"What were you doing here?" Fin asked.

"Taking pictures for a computer drawing I'm doing of old warehouses."

Cameron breathed another sigh of relief when she didn't mention law enforcement. Good girl; smart thinking.

Cameron walked back over to her. "Did you know we'd be here?"

Sophia shook her head, staring at the ground. Cameron grabbed her chin and forced her to look up at him—more theatrics for Fin and the guys' benefit, but Sophia was paying the price. "You had no idea we were here?"

"No," Sophia spat out. "I thought all these buildings were abandoned. I just needed some pictures." She was glaring at him, but Cameron could see the terror lurking just behind the anger.

"Yeah, I'm all for woman's lib, but I guess nobody would be stupid enough to send one tiny female with no backup or weapons to arrest all of us." Cameron leered at her. "No offense, sweetheart."

"Marco, did you find any ID on her?" Fin asked.

"Her purse was in her car, which was sitting out front. I moved the car inside the building just in case someone else drove by," Marco informed them.

Well, that answered the question about why Sophia's car hadn't been out front when Cameron had looked the second time.

Marco brought the purse to Fin. Fin glanced inside the bag, evidently finding nothing of interest, pulled out her wallet and let the purse fall to the ground. Fin took her driver's license out.

"Sophia Reardon. Twenty-seven years old. Alexandria

address." Fin looked through the rest of her wallet. Cameron held his breath, knowing Sophia must have some sort of FBI identification, even if she wasn't an agent. But Fin didn't say anything, just dropped her wallet into the purse on the ground.

Cameron thought of the card Sophia had slipped to him when he was searching her. Feigning as if he was looking around, Cameron slipped the card out of his pocket and glanced at it. Sure enough, Sophia's FBI credentials.

A smart and gutsy move on her part—one that had just saved her life. If Fin had seen FBI anywhere on her or in her possessions, they wouldn't have cared if she was just a graphic artist and not an agent. As far as they were concerned, anybody employed by the Bureau was their enemy.

Cameron caught Sophia's eye. He patted his pocket and gave her a slight nod. He had no idea if she understood what he was communicating, but she had done a good job.

Cameron walked over to Fin and leaned back against the SUV, knowing he had to play it casual. "So what do we do with her?"

Fin didn't answer immediately. That wasn't encouraging.

The hardest part of undercover work—especially in a situation like this—was figuring out how far you could take your bluff. Pull out of the game too soon and lose eight months of undercover work with only a couple of low-level arrests. But play the game too long and take a chance of somebody calling your bluff...

Which in this case would end in Sophia's death before Cameron could stop it.

And this situation was all the more complicated due to this new damn Ghost Shell technology DS-13 had. If Cameron blew his cover now, Omega would be hard-pressed to acquire that technology before it went on the black market. That could result in the loss of thousands of lives.

But Cameron wasn't going to let Sophia die. Not here. Not today. He was leaning very casually against the SUV, but he had slipped the safety off on his weapon, although it remained concealed under his shirt.

But just like Cameron, everyone here had a weapon. If this came down to a firefight, the odds were definitely not in his favor.

"Let's just let her go, Fin," Marco said. "Smash the camera, break her phone, slash her tires so she can't get anywhere. By the time she walks to the nearest phone, we'll be long gone."

Cameron could've hugged the big lug. That was exactly the suggestion he had wanted to make, but couldn't.

Fin looked over at Cameron, but Cameron just shrugged as if it didn't matter to him a bit what happened to Sophia.

"No," Fin finally said. "No loose ends. Kill her."

Cameron heard Sophia's indrawn breath and he looked over at her. Full-blown panic was visible in her eyes now. She looked as if she was about to make a run for it. Cameron hoped she wouldn't. He didn't think he could take out all four of the other men before someone got a shot off at her.

A quick plan came to Cameron. God, he hoped this would work. He pushed himself away from the car lazily. "Aw, come on, Fin, can't I at least have a little fun with her first? Take her back to the house so there's something for me to do instead of looking at your ugly mugs all the time?" Cameron used his most cajoling tone.

That got a couple chuckles from the men, but Fin wasn't convinced.

"I thought you didn't like her?"

Cameron smiled easily. "I don't like cops." Cameron walked over to Sophia and trailed a finger along her collarbone, just above her breasts. "But her, knowing she's not a cop? Hmm."

Cameron licked his lips and moved closer to Sophia. She shuddered and stepped as far away from him as she could. A tear fell from the corner of her eye.

The guys all laughed at her reaction to him. Cameron pushed her back against the warehouse wall angrily, as if she had embarrassed him. "Well, obviously I'm going to have to teach her some manners. But I'm up to the task. Maybe I'll know some dirty jokes when I'm done." That got more laughs.

Fin shook his head. "She's too skinny for me. I prefer women with some meat on their bones."

Cameron grinned and reached out to stroke some of Sophia's hair. She wouldn't even look at him. "Plenty of meat for me."

The guys snickered. Fin looked down at his watch. "Whatever. Do what you want with her. I don't care," Fin told Cameron. "But she's your responsibility. And you have to get rid of her when you're done."

Cameron felt marginally better now that the immediate threat to Sophia's life seemed to have passed, and his undercover work was also relatively safe. But he was pretty sure the look in her eyes would haunt him the rest of his life.

One last finishing touch to the show. He grabbed Sophia by the nape of the neck and hauled her roughly against him. He brought his mouth down heavily on hers, and wrapped his other arm around her hips. For a moment Sophia did nothing, then without warning she exploded into furious action, pushing away from him and squirming in his grasp.

Cameron brought his lips up her jawline to her ear, holding her body firmly against his. Quietly, so no one could hear him but her, he whispered, "Whatever you do, don't let anyone know you know me."

Sophia was attempting so hard to get away from him, Cameron wasn't sure if she heard him. He hoped she did. He brought his lips back to hers. This time she bit his lip.

The men howled in laughter when Cameron jerked back from her.

"Ow, you little hellion. You're going to pay for that."

He grabbed her arm and dragged her to the car. Someone opened the door for them and Cameron all but threw her in, then climbed in after her. It broke his heart to see how Sophia scrambled as far away from him as she could get in the confines of the SUV.

He had saved their lives for now, but the danger was far from finished. And he hoped the trauma he'd dealt Sophia wasn't too much to repair.

Sophia was just trying to keep it together. She slid all the way over in the seat to try to get as far away from Cameron as possible. If she could've curled herself into a tiny ball, she would have.

Normally she didn't like being in the backseat of a vehicle, especially when there were no windows she could roll down. But right now her claustrophobia would just have to get in line behind all the other things her brain had to freak out about.

Like the fact that she had just been kidnapped by some gang that her ex-boyfriend seemed to be part of.

Except she didn't know if he was *really* part of it or not. Undercover.

It would answer a lot of questions if Cameron was working undercover. Like why he had tried to get her out of the warehouse and hadn't said anything about her FBI credentials.

Of course, it could also be that he was now a member of this organized crime group, or whatever it was, and just didn't want his ex-girlfriend's brains to get splattered all over the pavement.

So back to square one.

Sophia peeked over at Cameron to find him watching her with a decidedly malevolent look in his eyes. Sophia shuddered. That leering look was not something she had ever thought she would see from Cameron. Maybe he really was a criminal now. Sophia tried not to panic. If that look from Cameron was real, she was in big trouble.

But then Sophia glanced up and saw the leader guy, Fin, watching her and Cameron in the rearview mirror. Maybe Cameron suspected that they were being watched and was playing a role.

Undercover.

Please, please, please let him be working undercover.

After Cameron had told her to go, she had done exactly what he had asked: gone straight to her car. But when she had gotten to the door, her car wasn't there. The big guy— Marco?—was driving it inside. Sophia cursed herself for leaving the keys in it, but she had thought there was no one around for miles.

Sophia had tried to sneak outside without Marco seeing her, but hadn't managed it. The next thing she knew he'd grabbed her and had dragged her out the back exit of the warehouse.

Where Cameron had proceeded to scream at, strike and humiliate her.

And maybe save her life.

Sophia touched her lip—it still hurt, both from the slap and his mouth-grinding kiss. She had no such misconception that she was really any safer now than she had been while at the warehouse. But at least nobody had a gun in their hands now.

As the men around her chatted and generally insulted each other, Sophia tried to watch out the window without looking as if she was watching out the window. She didn't want to give anyone—Cameron included—a reason to think she was a threat. But if she had a chance to get away, she planned to take it, and knowing where she was would help.

They were still pretty far outside of DC when they turned into a residential area. Definitely not high-end, the houses were old, but pretty large. They were far enough apart that neighbors wouldn't be forced to see what the other was doing unless they were deliberately trying to. All in all, probably a good location for people selling drugs or weapons or whatever else. Although it wasn't too promising, maybe Sophia would be able to call for help when they parked and got out of the car, and someone would notice.

Their SUV pulled up to the house on the corner. Although the house was probably built in the 1960s, someone had obviously refurbished the garage door with a contemporary opener. The SUV pulled straight into the garage and the door shut quickly behind them.

Sophia bit back a sigh. So much for calling out to the neighbors for help.

Cameron's scary, black look was back. And even though she hoped he might be a good guy, Sophia was frightened. Everyone got out of the car, but Sophia couldn't force herself to move. She shrank back into the seat when Cameron reached for her.

"Get out here right now," Cameron told her through gritted teeth.

She could hear the other men laughing in the doorway. Fin called out, "Regretting your decision already, Cam?"

"I'm not regretting anything, but someone else is about to."

One of the other men whose name she didn't know offered to come help Cam get her out of the vehicle, listing in very crude detail what he would do to her while he was assisting.

Cameron glared at Sophia through narrowed eyes for a moment before calling back over his shoulder, "Actually, that sounds like a pretty good idea, Rick. Why don't you come on in here?"

Sophia immediately scooted over to Cameron and out the car door. All the men doubled over in malicious laughter in the doorway. Cameron grabbed her arm and dragged her forcefully out of the garage past the men, and toward the back of the house into what obviously was his bedroom. Sophia could still hear the other gang members laughing.

Once inside, Cameron turned and locked the door. Then Sophia watched, standing in the middle of the room, as he went over and grabbed a wooden chair that was leaning against the far wall. He dragged the chair to the door and propped it under the doorknob—added defense against anyone entering.

Cameron turned from the door and walked slowly over to Sophia. He stopped only when he was just inches from her. He reached up and touched the split on her lip.

They both winced.

"I'm sorry for everything that happened today, and everything that's going to happen tonight," he told her softly. "But right now I'm going to need you to scream like you're terrified out of your mind. Or else I'm going to have to force you to do it."

Chapter Four

Cameron wasn't sure if this situation could get much worse, but the look Sophia gave him made him think it probably could.

"Wh-what?" she stammered, backing away from him.

"Scream."

"Why?"

Cameron took a step toward her, closing the space between them again. "Look, Sophia, I don't want to hurt you. I really don't," he whispered close to her ear. "But those creeps out there have to think that there is something pretty terrible going on in here."

Sophia looked around the room frantically, as if trying to find a way to escape. A tear seeped from the corner of her eye.

Cameron grimaced. Unfortunately, tears weren't going to cut it in this case. He had to prove to the men in the rest of the house that there was a reason he had brought Sophia here.

One she wouldn't like.

Ultimately, the worse it seemed in here for her, the safer she would be from the other men.

"You have to scream. Yell. Call me names. Do something."

But Sophia just shook her head, looking around the

room, anywhere but at him. It was almost as if she was in shock. Which would be understandable.

"Need some help in there, Cam?" Somebody—it sounded like Rick—called out from the other side of the door.

Damn. "Everything's just fine," Cameron responded.

Cameron gripped Sophia's arms—hard—and shook her. "C'mon, Soph. Work with me. If they think you like it, they're going to want their chance."

She still just looked at him mutely. It honestly seemed beyond her ability to make any sort of sound whatsoever.

"Damn it, Soph." Cameron shook her again. "I need you to fight me like you did back at the warehouse. Before you knew it was me."

Then it occurred to Cameron what he needed to do. She had fought him like a wildcat in the warehouse. Not because she thought he was such a bad guy, but because she seemed so claustrophobic.

In his training and work for both the US Army Rangers and then Omega Sector, Cameron had been taught how to use perps' weaknesses against them. It was one of the reasons Cameron had excelled at undercover work—his ability to pinpoint fears of the enemy. And use those fears without mercy.

He never thought he'd be using that training and skill to manipulate the one woman he once thought he might spend the rest of his life with.

Cameron spun Sophia around and put his hand over her mouth as he had at the warehouse. She immediately tensed up and started struggling. When he didn't release her after a few moments she began fighting in earnest.

Cameron, protecting his face as best he could from her clawing hands, dragged her over to where the lone dresser stood in the sparse room. She kicked at it, causing it to hit up against the wall.

He could hear laughter from the other rooms.

Cameron removed his hand from her mouth.

"Let me go!" Sophia yelled as soon as his hand was gone. Cameron released her for just a moment and she flung herself around to face him, breaths sawing in and out of her chest.

This wasn't going to work. They couldn't hear her if his hand was over her mouth, but she didn't scream if it wasn't. Cameron looked around. The room had a tiny walk-in closet. Maybe that would be small enough to terrify her.

Cameron steeled himself against the thought of Sophia's terror. He stepped toward her and this time she did scream as he reached for her.

"No!"

His hand covered her mouth again. He could hear whistles and catcalls from outside the door.

"Just a couple more minutes, baby. Hang in there," he whispered into Sophia's ear as he dragged her toward the closet.

When Sophia realized where they were headed, she fought him harder than before. Panic took over. She got a good punch to his cheek before he could catch her arm. That was going to leave a mark. But he didn't let it stop him.

He caught the door with his foot and pushed it open. The closet was practically empty, just a couple of his shirts hanging in it. It wasn't big by any means, with barely enough room for two people, but it wasn't tiny. Only someone who really struggled with tight spaces would have a problem being in it for a short amount of time.

Cameron dragged the struggling Sophia into the enclosed space, keeping her back to his chest. He pulled the door closed with one hand and released her mouth with his other.

Sophia screamed as if she was terrified out of her mind. Which she was.

Cameron had no idea what obnoxious comments or noises the members of DS-13 were making about this. He couldn't hear anything over Sophia's screams.

Sophia fought in a violent frenzy—kicking, clawing, throwing wild punches. Cameron just tried to keep her from hurting him or herself. He kept her as close as he could to his body. After what seemed like the longest period of time in the history of the world—and probably even longer to her—but was really only a few seconds, Cameron opened the door and let go of Sophia. She immediately pushed away from Cameron and all but dived out of the closet, landing heavily on the floor.

She pushed herself across the floor, as far away from him and the closet as she could get, sucking in deep gulps of air the entire time. When she reached the far corner of the room she dragged her knees up to her chest and rocked back and forth. Cameron stood just outside the closet, watching her, unsure what to do. He had no idea why she was so claustrophobic, but it was definitely not something she had any control over.

In that moment Cameron hated every single thing about his life in law enforcement. He was here to catch bad guys. But right now the good guys were the ones who were paying the price.

Cameron took a step toward Sophia and she cringed away from him, whimpering. "No, please…" She stretched out her arms as if to ward him off.

"No," Cameron whispered. "I won't do that again. Never again."

Sophia nodded her head, but still shied away from him. Cameron didn't want to move any closer to her. She'd been through enough. Down the hall, Cameron could hear the

TV blaring. Evidently the guys thought the show in Cameron's room was over.

He hoped it had been worth it. Because looking at Sophia right now, Cameron didn't think there was any way it could possibly have been.

Cameron took a few steps toward her then sat down on the floor so he could be eye to eye with Sophia. Her breathing was still labored, and every last ounce of color was missing from her face.

"Sophia, I'm so sorry." Cameron spoke softly. He knew this room wasn't bugged, but couldn't take any chances on any member of DS-13 overhearing them.

Cameron moved a little closer to Sophia but she shied away again. Cameron rubbed the back of his neck, where permanent tension seemed to have lodged, at least since he had first seen Sophia again this afternoon.

He wanted to give Sophia the physical space she needed, but the things he needed to say couldn't be said from across the room. Moving slowly, he scooted over until he was next to her against the wall.

Sophia just huddled into her corner and didn't look at him. But at least her breathing was slowing down a bit, wasn't quite so labored.

"Sophia, I'm so sorry," he said again. As if saying it again would make everything okay. "I had to make them think that something bad was happening in here."

Sophia gave a quiet bark of acerbic laughter.

Cameron shook his head. "I mean, something *they* would think is bad. You know what they expected."

Sophia nodded her head slightly, but didn't say anything. They sat there in silence for long moments. Cameron tried to figure out what possible words could make this better.

"Things have changed since I saw you last, five years ago," Cameron said softly, close to her ear.

"I know," Sophia all but hissed, but just as softly. "The Cameron Branson I knew five years ago never would've done this." She gestured toward her face with her hand, then pointed toward the closet with a shaky arm.

"Sophia, I'm sorry I hit you earlier. I had to take action immediately. And the closet…" Cameron shrugged wearily. "It had to be done."

Sophia turned away from him again without saying anything.

"It's not like I planned any of this. Damn it, Soph, I'm just trying to keep you alive."

Sophia covered her face with her hands and began to cry. Looking over at the arm that was now exposed because her short-sleeved blue shirt was ripped at the shoulder, he could see some angry red marks on her arm. Those were from him, probably during the closet fiasco. They were definitely going to leave bruises on her pale skin, even though he had only been trying to help.

Although it pained him, Cameron hardened himself against the ache he felt at the thought of marring her beautiful skin. The bruises would help sell their story to DS-13.

"At least tell me you're here, you know…working," Sophia finally said to him.

Cameron appreciated that she left out the word *undercover*. That word could get them both killed quicker than almost anything else they could say. "Yeah. I'm with the agency."

Cameron knew he was being vague, but didn't think now was the time to go into Omega Sector and his life there. When they had known each other before, he had just been coming out of the Rangers. Sophia didn't know anything about Omega—even most people who worked in the FBI knew nothing about it.

Sophia let out a sigh and turned toward him slightly. "Well, that's a relief. I wasn't sure."

She wasn't sure? "Seriously? What did you think, I had left the Rangers and joined some sort of crime syndicate since we last spoke?"

"Stranger things have happened."

Cameron shook his head. "I guess." He must really have been undercover too long if an old friend couldn't tell if he was pretending or not. Maybe he had been in the darkness too long.

Cameron didn't have time for metaphors about darkness and light in his life. He had a job to do: justice for his partner's killer and retrieval of Ghost Shell. And now making sure Sophia got out of this alive and relatively unscathed.

He definitely did not have time to think about how beautiful she was, or how much she had meant to him five years ago, or how often he had thought about her since.

Keeping her alive. That was the most important thing.

WAS HE HONESTLY offended that she couldn't tell if he was really working undercover or not when she was sitting here with bruises and a racing heartbeat from what he had done to her?

Sophia looked at the closet again. From across the room, it looked so benign. Obviously there was plenty of air throughout both this room and the closet. She very clearly knew that now. But five minutes ago there had been no way to convince her mind of that.

She pulled her knees closer to her body. She believed Cameron when he said he was undercover. She even believed he was doing what he thought was best when he had hit her earlier, and everything that had happened since. But that didn't mean she wanted him to touch her again.

But part of her desperately wanted him to touch her

again. She had wanted that for five years. But not here in this house with those filthy men in the next room.

Sophia glanced sideways at Cameron. He looked as exhausted as she felt. Sophia didn't know much about undercover work, but she was sure that her entrance into the picture had to have thrown a wrench into whatever mission he was on.

"Have I totally screwed things up for you? I tried to get out of the warehouse like you said, but that big guy was out there," Sophia offered softly.

Cameron looked surprised that she was talking to him at all. Now that she was calming down she was realizing that Cameron really had been working in her best interest.

But she still wanted out of here as soon as possible.

"Well, your presence was definitely unexpected. But so far it looks like there was no harm done to the case."

"Really?" Sophia couldn't believe that was true.

"Yeah, evidently how I've been treating you has been helping solidify my bad-guy reputation."

"How long have you been…working with them?" Sophia turned toward him slightly.

"This group is called DS-13. They're basically into everything—weapons, drugs, money laundering. And now it looks like they're expanding into full-on terrorism." Cameron gestured toward the rest of the house with his thumb. "I've been in this house for about three weeks, but first made contact eight months ago."

"What do you do? I mean, what do they think you do?"

"They think I'm a midlevel weapons dealer. What you walked in on today was a sale I had set up."

Sophia shook her head. Just sheer bad luck. If Bruce had gotten the pictures when he was supposed to have… "If they did a sale, can't you make arrests?"

Cameron shifted a little closer to her, but this time Sophia didn't feel the need to move away.

"I could've arrested everybody there, and would've tried if things had gotten much more out of hand."

"Tried?"

Cameron reached over and pulled up her ripped sleeve, as if he could reattach it to the rest of her shirt by sheer will. "There were four of them, all armed, against just you and me. And only I had a weapon."

"Not very good odds, I guess." Sophia shuddered thinking about it.

"No, I doubt if either of us would've made it out alive." Cameron shrugged and smiled crookedly at her. "But I would've tried."

"Don't you have a wire or something? Backup?"

"Sometimes. But not in deep cover like this. It's too complicated and dangerous to have surveillance all the time. DS-13 is smart—that's why they chose this house. Surveillance vehicles would be pretty easy to spot around here."

"But what if you need help?" Sophia couldn't believe they would just send Cameron in by himself.

He smiled at her again and she found herself shifting a little more toward him.

That cocky smile. Lord, how she'd missed it.

"Honey, I can take care of myself. But I do have ways to bring in backup, if I need it."

"Like today?"

"Believe it or not, today was mostly for show. The buyers were picked up not long after they left the warehouse. The whole thing was just supposed to show DS-13 how helpful and well-organized my buys could be for them."

Cameron stretched his long legs out in front of him. "The agency was supposed to have blocked everything off so nobody would be around those warehouses."

Sophia rolled her eyes. "Yeah, well, I got way lost and ended up coming through some farmer's back field to get to the warehouses. If the FBI was watching the roads, that's why they didn't see me."

Cameron nodded as if she had just solved some puzzle for him. "I didn't want to make any arrests because these are just lower-level bad guys. I'm trying to get their boss."

Sophia watched, a little frightened, as Cameron's face and posture hardened right before her eyes. Whoever this "boss" was, Cameron wanted to take him down. Badly.

"No luck yet?"

"Haven't even met him. This sort of work is tricky—you can't push too hard or it backfires on you."

Sophia nodded. She couldn't imagine the sort of pressure being undercover would put on someone. Never knowing if you were making the right choices, or when you may be discovered.

It had definitely made Cameron Branson into a harder man than when she had known him five years ago. Then, he had still been strong—physically, mentally, in all possible ways. But now there was an edge to him that hadn't been there before. One that scared her a little.

One that had probably saved her life earlier.

Almost as if her body was moving of its own accord she turned toward him. He did look exhausted. His black hair, grown out from how short it used to be, was touching his collar. Before she could stop herself, Sophia reached out and tucked a stray curl back from where it had fallen onto his forehead, nearly to his eyes.

For a moment they looked at each other. Sophia forgot where they were, the danger they were in, the fear she had felt. She only saw Cameron.

Something slid under the door before a fist beat loudly

on it. Sophia jumped back at the sound, the moment—whatever it was—shattered.

"Cam, man, you alive in there? I need to talk to you."

Cameron stood up and walked over to pick up whatever had been slid under the door. "Yeah, Fin. I'll be right out."

Cameron walked back over to her, and reached his hand out to help her up. Sophia hesitated for just a moment before taking it. "What is it he put under the door?"

Cameron walked with her over to the edge of the bed then sat down with a sigh. He held up what was in his hands: plastic zip ties—used everywhere to secure and fasten all sorts of things.

Sophia shook her head, confused. What were the ties for? Whatever it was, Cameron wasn't too happy about it.

"Poor man's handcuffs," he finally said. "I guess Fin wants to make sure you don't try to escape or anything while he and I are talking."

Oh. "Okay, I guess." Sophia was determined to keep it together. Now that she knew Cameron was undercover, she needed to help him if she could. Not being hysterical was the most help she could offer right now.

"Just don't try to struggle against them. They'll cut into your wrists if you do."

Sophia swallowed hard and nodded.

"I'm going to run one set around your wrists and one around your ankles since there's nothing in this room to secure you to. It will look more authentic that way if someone checks."

Sophia's panicked glaze flew up to his. Someone checking?

A fist pounded on the door again. "Damn it, Cam. Hurry up. You can finish doing whatever you want to her after we talk."

Cameron spoke to her quickly as he pulled the plastic

fasteners around her ankles. "I'll be as fast as I can, but sometimes Fin likes to hear himself talk."

Cameron tightened the ties so they were tight but not painful. "If anybody comes through that door that isn't me, start screaming your head off. Immediately. Don't wait to see what they want."

Sophia nodded. That wasn't a problem. She knew her screaming voice was definitely in working condition.

Cameron slipped the other ties around her wrists, and pulled them tight. He helped her so she was sitting up against the wall the bed leaned against.

Cameron leaned down and put his forehead against hers. "I'm going to get you out of this. I swear to God." He lowered his lips and kissed her gently, then turned and strode out of the room without another word.

Chapter Five

Obnoxious catcalls met Cameron as he walked down the hall and past the living room. He stopped and gave the guys a little smirk and bow—even though it made him sick to his stomach—before turning and heading into the kitchen to see Fin.

Fin sat at the table, nursing a beer. Cameron made his way to the fridge to get a beer of his own as Fin looked him up and down.

"Worth it?" the man asked.

Cameron gave his most sly smile. "Absolutely." He held his beer up in silent salute as he took the seat across from Fin.

Fin gestured toward Cameron's face. "Looks like she may have given you a bruise there on your cheek."

He thought of all the marks on Sophia's arms. "She'll have plenty of her own."

Fin cackled at that. "Well, I'm glad it was worth the trouble." Cameron settled back in his chair, somehow managing to keep the smile on his face.

"So, I spoke to Mr. Smith tonight, while you were having your…fun," Fin continued.

Cameron kept his best poker face and feigned disinterest as he took a sip from his bottle. "I didn't know Mr. Smith was interested in the details of that sort of fun."

"Mr. Smith is interested in anything and everything that has to do with DS-13. And he has taken an interest in you."

Bingo. Eight months undercover, and this was what he had been waiting for. "Oh, yeah? Why's that?"

"He was impressed—has always been impressed—with how the sales you arrange go down without a hitch."

Cameron nodded and took a sip of his beer. "That's what I do."

"Well, Mr. Smith would like for you to start arranging more meetings and perhaps find some other sorts of buyers for some items he's come into recently."

"What sort of items?" Encoding technology, perhaps?

"Mr. Smith wants to meet you and tell you about that himself."

Cameron could tell Fin was watching him closely to see how he would react. How he played this off would be key. Too much enthusiasm would most certainly be reported back to Mr. Smith, and perhaps cause the whole invitation to be pulled. Not enough enthusiasm would be reported back as an insult.

But insult was definitely better than suspicion, so Cameron took another long drag on his beer and remained sprawled in his chair.

"That's cool. Whatever. Just let me know when." Cameron yawned, then got up, as if the meeting with Fin was over. He could tell Fin wasn't expecting that.

"Whoa, hang on there a minute, Cam. I'm not done."

"Oh…sorry, man." Cameron sat back down as if he didn't really care much about what Fin was going to say next. Which couldn't be further from the truth.

"Mr. Smith wants to meet you *tomorrow*," Fin told him.

That was a little sooner than Cameron expected, but not too bad. If he could find a way to get Sophia to safety.

"Okay, that's fine. Is he coming here? Does he want me

to set up something with a buyer for tomorrow? That's kind of hard when I don't know what he's selling."

Fin shook his head. "No, he only wants to meet you tomorrow. Let's just say that your actions with the pretty brunette have reassured him that you're not afraid of getting your hands a little dirty."

Cameron grinned despite his souring stomach. "Well, it wasn't my hands getting dirty, if you know what I mean."

Fin howled in laughter again before turning serious. "Mr. Smith needs you to begin setting up some meetings with people who may be interested in doing a little bit more damage than just with a few automatic weapons."

"You mean like missiles or something?"

"No, actually a specific computer program or virus or something that can do major damage to law enforcement. I don't really understand it. But Mr. Smith says it's going to bring in a lot of money."

Cameron nodded. "Okay, man, no problem. Tell Mr. Smith I can line that up for him."

"Actually, you can tell him yourself when you see him tomorrow. He's having a bit of a get-together at his mountain home. Has some people he'd like you to meet."

Crap. "Mountain home? Where? And I don't think it's going to work real well to bring 'my companion' on a plane, you know?"

"Cam, DS-13's resources are much greater, and more organized, than you think. We'll be using a small jet, owned by one of DS-13's dummy corporations. And Mr. Smith's house is in the mountains of Virginia."

"Wow. I didn't know about all that." Actually, Cameron did know about all that, at least all of it except the mountain house. No wonder Smith was never spotted, since he had some sort of secluded retreat.

Damn it. All of this just got much harder for him and

Omega Sector. He needed to contact them tonight and let them know about the location change.

But most important he needed to get Sophia out of here as soon as possible. There was no way he was going to let her be transported to some remote location where he had even less control over the situation.

"There's a lot you don't know about DS-13, Cam," Fin said, smiling knowingly, self-importance fairly radiating off him. "Just be ready to go in the morning. We'll have to figure out what to do with your little friend by then."

"Private jet. Cool." At least Cameron's cover persona would think so. Cameron himself didn't give a damn.

"You'll want to be at your best when you meet Mr. Smith," Fin told him with a grin. "So don't exhaust yourself with other things."

"Roger that." Cameron took the last sip of his beer and stood up. "See you tomorrow." As he walked out of the kitchen he grabbed a bag of chips and one of the post-workout protein shakes the guys had lying around. It wasn't a great meal for Sophia, but at least it was something.

Cameron didn't have much time. Morning would come fast. He had no doubt that when Fin said they'd "figure out what to do with" Sophia in the morning, he meant kill her. He had to think of a plan to get Sophia out of here. Quickly.

Cameron walked as casually as he could back to the room. As he opened the door, he saw Sophia, still tied as he had left her, about to start screaming.

"It's just me." He put down the food and walked quickly over to her. "Are you okay? Any problems?"

"No, I'm fine. Just ready to get untied."

Cameron pulled out the knife he always kept in his pocket. He made quick work of the zip ties, first at her wrists then her ankles, allowing the plastic to drop to the floor.

Sophia rubbed her wrists to try to get some of the blood to flow back normally. Cameron reached down and gently rubbed her ankles.

"Better?" he asked softly.

Sophia nodded. "Yeah, thanks. Did everything go okay out there?"

Cameron reluctantly stopped rubbing her ankles, released her feet and went to put the chair back under the door handle. He handed her the food and she began to eat.

He turned to her. "Yes and no."

Sophia drew her knees up to her chest and wrapped her arms around them. "Yes and no? That doesn't sound too good."

Cameron came and sat back down on the edge of the bed. "Well, in a rather ironic turn of events, it seems that the horrible way I've treated you has made DS-13 trust me more."

"What?"

"Whatever doubts they had about me have evidently been eradicated since I have turned into a rapist slimeball."

"But you didn't…"

"Yeah, but they don't know that. Evidently your screams were pretty convincing." Cameron rubbed an exhausted hand over his eyes. He didn't want to think about that again.

Sophia unwrapped her grip on her legs and crawled a little closer to him, reaching out and touching him on the arm. "Cam, you did what you had to do. I thought about it while you were gone. You saved both of our lives without a doubt."

"Sophia…"

She moved a little closer. "I'm sorry about all that stuff I said. I don't think badly of you. I can't stand you thinking badly of yourself."

Cameron turned so he was facing directly toward her. He took the hand that was touching his arm and held it in both of his. God, she was so sweet. He looked down at the hand in his—so tiny.

He couldn't stand the thought of her being in this room— around these people—a minute longer. And the thought of taking Sophia to that other house where Mr. Smith was? Totally unacceptable.

Cameron reached out and stroked her cheek. She was looking at him so intently, so concerned about his *feelings*. Cameron could barely remember the last time he'd had an authentic feeling. Until today.

"I'm fine, Soph. If anything, just glad that something good has come out of this situation."

She smiled shyly before easing away. "Me, too."

"It seems that the quite elusive leader of DS-13, a man named Mr. Smith, wants to meet me now because of how everything went down today."

"That's good, right?"

Cameron nodded and eased backward on the bed so he was sitting next to her. "Yeah. That's what I've been try- ing to do for eight months."

"So what's the bad?"

Cameron sighed. "He wants to meet me tomorrow."

Cameron watched as Sophia obviously tried to figure out what that meant for her. "Oh, okay," she finally responded.

"Even worse, he wants for me to go to his mountain house. That's not…optimal for the situation."

"Because of me?"

"Partially, but not totally. I wasn't aware of this other location until tonight. I don't know anything about it so it's hard to prepare for it."

Sophia nodded, worry plain in her eyes.

He didn't know if she was worried for herself or him. Probably both. "But you're not going, so you don't need to worry about anything."

"I'm not going?"

"We're going to get you out of here tonight."

Sophia sat up straighter, obviously ready for action. "We are? How?"

"Wait until late, when everyone is asleep, then I'm going to tell you how to sneak out."

"But won't that cause trouble for you? Won't your cover be blown?"

Cameron shook his head. "Not if we do it right. It's going to have to look like you knocked me unconscious. I'm going to need a pretty good goose egg on my head."

When Sophia just shook her head, Cameron continued, "If anything, it will help. They'll be in a panic that you'll call the cops and will want to get out of here even faster. Anything that throws them off their timetable can only help me."

"That's good, I guess." Sophia shook her head again. "But I don't want to hit you with anything."

Cameron reached up and softly touched her swollen and bruised lip. "C'mon sweetie, turnabout is fair play."

"Cameron." Sophia reached up and touched his hand. "You did this because you had to. I know that."

"And you'll do this because you have to. It's the only way, Sophia."

Sophia didn't like it. She really had come to terms with what he had done while he was having his meeting with Fin. Everything that had happened from the moment she had seen Cameron in the warehouse today had been done to protect her.

She didn't want to hurt him. But it looked as if she was going to have to.

"There's no other way?" she asked.

"Not if we want to keep suspicions off me. I'll wake up

and notice you're gone. Then I'll tell everyone we should leave before you call the cops."

"They won't think you let me go?"

Cameron shook his head. "Absolutely not. Especially not after earlier. Although can you do something for me?"

"I can try."

Cameron leaned close and whispered in her ear, "Can you yell, 'Get off me, you bastard'? It's been a little too quiet in here."

Sophia shot off the bed. If she couldn't do it, would he drag her back into the closet? She looked over at it, then back at him.

Cameron wasn't making moves toward her—as a matter of fact, he was keeping himself very casual and relaxed on the bed—but Sophia still took a step back. Then she stopped.

Just yell. It's not hard. Just do it.

"Get off me, you bastard!" she yelled at the top of her voice.

Immediately she could hear guffaws of laughter from other places in the house. Perverts.

Cameron got off the bed and came to stand right next to her. "Thank you."

"Anything to stay out of the closet."

Cameron grinned. "Got it." He grabbed her hand and brought it up to his lips and kissed it softly.

They both seemed a little shocked by his impulsive gesture, but Sophia didn't pull her hand away and Cameron didn't let it go.

"I just want to get you out of here. That's the most important thing to me," Cameron whispered. He let go of her hand, wrapped his arms around her and drew her to his chest. Sophia snuggled in. After what she had been through today his arms felt like absolute heaven. This was what she remembered about them from five years ago: a closeness that matched the burning attraction between them.

She and Cameron had met at a diner that was just a couple of blocks from her tiny apartment in Washington, near Georgetown University, where she went to school. Hating her own cooking, Sophia had made a habit of going to the diner each morning and one particularly crowded day Cameron had asked to share her booth and they'd struck up a conversation. Then he had started showing up at the same time every morning, displaying a great deal of interest in her.

Emotionally, Sophia had fallen fast and she had fallen hard.

But physically, Sophia was shy and a little bit awkward, so she had taken things slowly with Cameron, thinking they would have all the time in the world. For three months, they went on dates, shared many passionate kisses, sometimes talked all night, just to end up back at the diner for breakfast the next morning.

Sophia had thought—had *known*—Cameron was the one for her. And his willingness to wait so patiently for her physically had made her love him even more.

And she thought he felt the same way. But then one morning he didn't show up. The thought still left her feeling a little sick to her stomach. Plus, he had waited until he knew she would be at the diner to call her home phone and leave a message. *Hi, Soph. Something's come up and I'm going to have to leave town permanently. I wish you all the best. Take care.*

She still knew the message by heart. At least now, five years later, she didn't cringe when she thought about it.

Sophia eased herself back from his arms. A nice hug in the middle of a traumatic event was one thing, allowing herself to dive into the past and drag out all the hurts was quite another.

Cameron didn't try to hold on to her when Sophia pulled back. And although she knew it was for the best, it still panged her just a little.

"Okay, so what's the plan?" Sophia asked as she moved away and sat back down on the bed, which was as sparse as everything else in this room. She looked around. Nothing was inviting or comforting in the least. And the little she'd seen of the rest of the house as he'd dragged her in here wasn't much better.

Plus it was pretty stuffy in here. There was only a tiny window, covered by cheap blinds that barely let in any light at all. The bedroom was attached to a bathroom, but that room wasn't much more appealing, even with its own window.

Cameron saw her looking around. "What?"

"Just…this room. This entire house. You've been here three weeks, you said? How can you stand it?"

Cameron shrugged. "It's just part of the job. DS-13 wanting me to stay here was actually a huge step in the right direction. It meant they were really starting to trust me. Took long enough."

"Eight months, right? Isn't that a long time for—" she lowered her voice even further "—undercover work? Consistent work?"

"Yeah, it's starting to reach the outer limits. But I asked to stay on this case and keep this cover for so long."

"Why?"

Cameron came and sat next to Sophia on the bed. "Let's just say that I'm determined that Mr. Smith—leader of DS-13—is going down."

Fierce determination gleamed in Cameron's eyes, as well as frustration.

"Something in particular you want him for, or just because he's a really bad guy?" Sophia asked, wanting to understand.

"Him being a bad guy is enough, but yeah, for me it's personal. He killed my partner last year. Viciously."

Sophia had no idea what to say to that. She reached out and touched his arm. "I'm so sorry, Cam."

Cameron nodded. "Mr. Smith suspected Jason, my partner, was undercover. Then cut his throat when he found out it was true."

Sophia's expression shuttered and she rubbed Cam's arm. No wonder Cameron was so intent on arresting Mr. Smith. She didn't blame him.

Cameron stood, and Sophia's hand fell away. "I will get him, Soph. Don't doubt it."

"I don't." Sophia smiled at Cameron and stood up. "So how are we getting me out of your way so you can get your job finished? Because, honestly, I can't stand the thought of you living in this jackass-infested rat hole much longer." She gestured around the room with her hand.

Cameron chuckled softly. "Jackass-infested rat hole?"

Sophia raised one eyebrow. "Seems apt. Although perhaps my metaphor is a bit mixed. I just want to get out of here and let you get to the other evil lair."

Cameron chuckled again. "I'm pretty sure they don't call it an evil lair."

Sophia smiled. She had missed his laugh. "Well, they should. So what's the plan?"

They were both startled by a loud pounding on the door again. Whoever it was tested the doorknob to see if it was locked. Cameron hooked his arm around Sophia and pulled her behind him so he was between her and the door.

"I'm busy in here!" Cameron yelled out, making annoyance plain in his voice. "What the hell do you want?"

"Cam, Fin said to give you these." It was one of the men, but Sophia didn't know which one. More plastic ties slid under the door.

"Fine, Rick. But stay the hell out unless you're trying to see my naked ass, you pervert."

They heard Rick mutter something about wanting to see a naked ass, but not Cameron's. But at least he left them alone. If Rick decided to force his way through the door, that chair propped under the knob definitely wasn't going to stop him.

Cameron breathed a sigh of relief when he seemed sure Rick was gone. "We've definitely got to get you out of here."

A thought occurred to Sophia. "Why did you tell them your real name? Isn't that dangerous?"

"They only know my first name. I discovered a while ago that it was better to use my first name for covers. Less confusion, less possible mistakes."

Sophia wasn't sure she understood. "Mistakes?"

"Well, if bad guys think your name is Tom but some complete stranger happens to say the name Cameron and you react…"

"Game over."

Cameron nodded. "Game definitely over. It's easier to keep the lies as close to the truth as possible."

"But no Branson, right?"

"Nope. Cam Cameron, at your service."

Sophia rolled her eyes. "Cam Cameron?"

Cameron shrugged. "Hey, it works."

"All right, Cam Cameron, what do we do now?"

"Now we climb in bed and wait a few hours, so I can get you out of here as soon as everyone's asleep. You need to be long gone before tomorrow morning."

Chapter Six

Lying in bed with Cameron for the few hours before they were going to sneak her out, Sophia never would've thought she would sleep. But evidently her traumatized mind had other plans.

Cameron had lain down with her on the small bed and tucked her into his side.

"Try to rest, if you can," he had whispered.

The last thing Sophia remembered was snorting, "Yeah, right." The next thing she knew, Cameron was waking her up…

With a kiss.

It took her a moment to figure out what was happening. Even longer to remember where she was. But she shut that all out for a few moments and melted into Cameron.

Sophia twisted in the tiny bed so she could get closer to him. She wrapped her fingers in his hair and pulled him against her. Cameron's hand slid from her neck all the way down her back and splayed out over her hip. He pulled her closer and deepened the kiss.

Sophia could barely keep from moaning. She had missed this passion between them that erupted without either of them being able to do anything about it.

Cameron's lips trailed from her mouth, over her jaw and

down to her neck. Sophia shivered, her breath quickening. She gave herself over to the sensation.

But after a few moments Cameron pulled away.

"I'm sorry, Soph. I shouldn't have done that."

Suddenly, all the reasons why this wasn't a good idea came crashing back to her. Sophia jerked away from him.

"You're right. You shouldn't have done that."

Cameron sighed and got up from the bed.

"I think everyone is asleep. It's time for us to get you out of here."

Sophia decided to let go of her annoyance about the kiss. Kisses. Complete make-out session. Whatever. There were more important things to concentrate on here.

She got up from the bed. "What time is it?"

"About 4:00 a.m. It's late enough that nobody should be awake, but still dark enough for you not to be seen."

Sophia nodded. "Okay. What do I need to do?"

"I'm going to walk you out and show you where the side door is. We'll go ahead and unlock it."

Sounded easy enough. "Okay."

"Once you get out, I want you to run, as fast as you can. When you get to the main road, there's a gas station about half a mile down. Call the Bureau and have somebody pick you up."

"No 911?"

"No. That would wreak havoc on what I'm doing here. I want them to think you've called 911, but I don't want to have to deal with any uniforms poking around."

Sophia nodded.

"After I show you the door," Cameron continued, "we have to come back in here. I can't hit myself hard enough for it to be realistic."

Sophia cringed. She didn't know if she'd be able to hit him hard enough, either.

Cameron opened the door and ushered Sophia out. Everything in the house was quiet. Cameron led her silently down the hall to the side door, past the garage. She watched as he unlocked the door, and cracked it just the slightest bit, so it wouldn't make any noise when she came out here in a few minutes.

Cameron turned and looked at Sophia. Sophia nodded. She knew what to do when she came back. They silently headed back toward Cameron's room. With every step, Sophia was terrified someone would wake up and catch them.

Would that mean death for both of them? Would Cameron be able to cover for them again? Sophia didn't know.

She was also concerned that he wouldn't be able to convince DS-13 that her escape was an accident. That he wouldn't be able to talk his way out of it and that all his time working undercover would go to waste.

Or worse.

Back in his room, Sophia turned to Cameron. "What if they don't believe I attacked you and got away? What if they think you let me go?"

Cameron put his hands on her forearms. "Soph, it's okay. I've been with them a long time. They'll believe me."

"But how will I know you're okay? How will I know something bad hasn't happened to you?"

Cameron's hands slid up from her arms, over her shoulders until they were framing her face. "I'm good at what I do. I'll make them believe me, don't worry."

Sophia nodded. Her hands were a little shaky as she asked, "Is this the part where I get to knock you unconscious?"

Cameron grimaced. "Yeah. You're going to need to use the butt of my SIG to hit me with. There's nothing else in here that will do."

Sophia didn't like the thought of hitting him, and liked

the thought of using a gun even less. "I don't know if that's a good idea. I don't know anything about guns."

"Well, just don't point it at me and pull the trigger and we'll be fine." Cameron's smile didn't reassure Sophia much. "I'll make sure it's not loaded," he added at her worried look. "Once you've hit me, take the gun with you and go. You probably won't even knock me unconscious. All that matters is that it looks like you did. In about an hour, I'll stumble out and wake everybody up, pretending like you just got away a few minutes ago."

Sophia had to admit, it was a pretty well-thought-out plan. She prayed it would work. For both their sakes.

"Okay, where do I hit you?" she whispered.

"On the back of the head, toward the base of my skull. Contrary to what you might think, it's the sudden, jerking motion of the skull that causes blackouts from an injury like this. Not necessarily the actual force."

"You mean I could hit you as hard as I can and it wouldn't matter?"

Cameron quickly corrected her. "No, that would definitely cause brain damage or possibly death. You don't want to rabbit-punch me."

"Rabbit punch is bad?"

Cameron nodded. "Very. I just mean that you don't necessarily need tremendous force to knock someone unconscious. It's the motion that causes it."

Sophia wasn't sure if she could do it. Cameron could see her obvious hesitation. "Soph, I'll be fine. But we're out of time. I need you to do this and get going."

Sophia nodded.

"I have a hard head, sweetheart. I've been swearing that was true every day for five years."

Sophia couldn't help but laugh softly. "You and me both."

Cameron sat on the bed, facing away from her. Sophia ran her fingers through his thick black hair, then let it go. She raised her arm with the gun in her hand.

"Ready?" Cameron asked. "Remember, hit me hard. Having to do it twice would really hurt. And once you've hit me, go. Don't wait around. I promise I will be fine. One, two, three."

Sophia brought the gun's handle down—hard—against the base of his skull. Cameron made a sickening groan and fell forward onto the bed. Sophia could see that he was still breathing. Blood was slowly seeping from a giant knot where she'd hit him. Tears slid down her cheeks as she glanced at Cameron once more before easing out the door of his room.

Sophia's breath seemed unimaginably loud to her as she made her way down the hallway as Cameron had shown her. Every step was full of terror, as she was afraid someone might wake up and catch her. As she walked through the kitchen, her shoes sounded so loud she slipped them off and carried them. Finally she made it to the side door that led outside from the kitchen.

It was closed.

Sophia knew Cameron had left that door open. She spun around in a panic, expecting to see someone behind her. But no one was there.

Maybe it had closed on its own. Sophia tried the knob. It was still unlocked. It must have just caught some wind or something. Regardless, she couldn't let it stop her now.

Sophia eased the door open as quietly as she could, grimacing with every little sound the door made. When the door was open the barest amount for her to fit, she slipped through, and pulled it gently and slowly closed behind her.

Sophia breathed a silent sigh of relief. At least she was out of the house. She bent down to put her flats back on her feet and took a deep breath to get her bearings and get ready to run. That's when she smelled it: cigarette smoke.

From right around the corner of the house.

Sophia quickly moved behind a large trash can that sat against the house, in case whoever was there came around the corner. Now she wouldn't be able to run the way Cameron had directed without being seen. She'd have to go the opposite way and then double back to the gas station when she was farther away from the house.

"I don't understand why we have to stay up all night." It sounded like Rick, the mean one with cold eyes.

"Well, you know Fin's not going to stay up if we're going to see Mr. Smith tomorrow."

Sophia didn't really care about who had to stay up or why Fin needed his beauty rest to see Mr. Smith. She needed to get out of here, now.

"But I don't understand why Fin doesn't trust Cam. Cam's one of us." That sounded like the big guy, Marco.

Sophia was starting to ease her way around to the back of the house when she heard Marco's statement. Fin didn't trust Cameron? She stopped and eased her way back so she could hear the conversation better.

"Yeah, well, if the woman is still here in the morning, then we'll know Cam is on the up-and-up. But like Fin said, if Cam let the woman get away…" Rick's voice trailed off.

"That doesn't mean he's a cop."

"He's either a cop or someone who lets a hundred-pound woman get the jump on him. Either way, DS-13 doesn't want him. Fin will take care of that." Rick laughed and Marco joined in after a moment.

Damn it. Sophia realized she was, in essence, signing Cameron's death warrant if she left now. She couldn't do it. She would have to sneak back inside and they'd figure out something else. She needed to hurry back into Cameron's room before he came out and told everyone she was missing.

And got himself killed.

Sophia peeked around the side of the trash can and jerked herself back as the two men walked around the corner. She held her breath, praying they hadn't seen her.

Marco was talking about a football game coming on that night as they walked in the kitchen door. Sophia felt her heart drop as she heard the click of the lock once they were inside.

She had to find a way back into the house. Sophia ran around to the back, having to make her way over a low wooden fence when she found the fence gate locked. From the back of the house in the dark, it was hard to tell which room was Cameron's.

Sophia knew she had to figure it out quickly. Cameron was running out of time and he had no idea about it.

Sophia definitely didn't want to climb into the wrong room. But one window was a little higher than the others, and smaller. That must be the bathroom, which would make Cameron's the window to the left.

Sophia ran to Cameron's window and began tapping on it. She had to get his attention before he went out and told them she was gone. She tapped as loud as she dared, not wanting to wake anyone else.

"Cameron?" Sophia cupped her hands to the window in an attempt to make the sound go through it, rather than out. "Cameron!"

Nothing. She rapped on the pane again but he didn't come to the window. Sophia tried to open the window but it was locked from the inside.

She had to get in the house. It might already be too late.

Sophia climbed up onto the air-conditioning unit so she

could reach the small window of the bathroom. Someone had left it cracked, just a little bit, but it was enough.

Sophia got her hands under the frame and slid it up as high as it would go, cringing as it made a loud creaking sound. She hefted her body up and into the tiny opening. All the buttons of her blouse ripped off as she scooted through, but Sophia didn't stop. When a nail caught her shoulder Sophia let out a cry, but still didn't stop.

She finally got herself through the opening and fell into the bathtub on the other side. She got up as quickly as she could, using a towel to wipe the blood from a pretty large gash on her shoulder. She rushed into Cameron's room.

But he wasn't there.

Chapter Seven

The crack Sophia gave him on the back of the head definitely wasn't too soft. Although Cameron didn't lose consciousness for more than a few seconds—at least he didn't think so—his head hurt like the devil. Lying on his bed doing nothing, giving Sophia time to get away before he "discovered" her gone, was no problem.

After a few minutes he decided to get out of the bed and make his way out into the main part of the house. Nobody should be awake yet, and being caught knocked senseless would look better out in the living room than lying in his bed.

The room spun dizzyingly as Cameron got up. He couldn't hold back a groan. He felt as if sirens were going off in his head, and on top of that he could swear he heard someone calling his name. Maybe Sophia hit him harder than he thought.

Cameron ignored the pain and started out his door. After a few steps at least the building stopped spinning. He stumbled—mostly not acting—out into the living room.

Where both Marco and Rick sat, wide-awake.

This was not good. Why were they awake and dressed? How had Sophia gotten by them?

Cameron tried to silently move back into his room, but Rick saw him.

"What's going on, Cameron?" Rick asked him.

Cameron had no idea how to play this off. Did they already have Sophia? "My head. That bitch hit me on the head."

Cameron watched as Marco and Rick looked at one another pointedly. Another not-good sign. Something was going on here that Cameron didn't know. He decided not to mention Sophia being gone yet. Give her as much time as possible.

"What are you guys doing up?" Cameron plopped down on the couch and gritted his teeth as the back of his head throbbed. Better play off the head injury until he knew what was going on.

"We're just up. Getting everything ready to go to the other house," Marco told him.

"At like—what time is it?—five o'clock in the morning?" Cameron saw Marco and Rick make that weird eye contact again. Something was definitely not right.

"Where is the woman?" The voice came from behind Cameron on the couch. Fin.

Cameron racked his brain for what to say now. To say she had just hit him and run obviously wasn't going to cut it. He had no idea how he was going to get out of this.

"In my room. She hit me on the head with a bottle and I clocked her. I used one of the plastic ties on her hands and threw her in the closet."

Cameron stood up and walked toward the kitchen. Maybe they wouldn't look for her and wouldn't notice she was gone for a while. It would give him a chance to get out or at least get to one of the other weapons in his room.

"Marco, go get her," Fin told the bigger man.

Damn it. Cameron shrugged and kept walking toward the kitchen as casually as he could. He wondered if his partner, Jason, had faced some sort of situation like this.

Feeling the walls closing in on you and knowing there was no way out.

Knowing unless there was some sort of miracle, you were going to die.

Marco came back into the kitchen. "She's not in the closet, boss."

Rick and Marco both pulled out their guns and pointed them directly at Cameron.

"Whoa, what the hell's going on here?" Feigned shock was Cameron's only option. "It's too early in the morning for this. What are you pointing them at me for?"

Fin pulled out a wicked-looking blade. Cameron knew how much pride the smaller man took in it. He suspected it was the same knife that had killed his partner.

"Where's the woman, Cam?" Fin asked, walking closer.

"I told you, I threw her in the closet."

Fin looked over at Marco, who shook his head. "She's not in the closet."

"Fine, she's not in the closet. Maybe she's under the bed or something. Everybody knows Marco can't find his keys half the time. No surprise he can't find a person, either."

Cameron got up and strolled purposely to his room, as if to prove Marco wrong about Sophia. He knew taking them by surprise in there would be his best option.

The best of really, really bad options. Two guns and a knife against his bare hands and the very slight element of surprise?

Cameron entered his room, thankful that at least Sophia had gotten away. He walked over to his closet and thrust open the door.

"See? Told you," Marco said.

"Screw you, Marco." Cameron still kept up the innocent act. "She's in here somewhere."

Cameron looked under his bed, hoping to find anything there that could be used as a weapon. Nothing.

He got back up. It looked as if the guys were relaxing just a little bit. Good.

Cameron walked toward the bathroom door. "You check in there, Marco?"

Marco looked sheepish. "No." The big man looked over at Fin.

"Check it out," Fin told him.

This would be Cameron's only chance. Marco's back would be to him. He'd have to take down Rick first, since he had the gun. And Fin's knife was nothing to scoff at.

Cameron took a deep breath and tried to center himself. He ignored any pain in his head and focused on making it through the next few seconds alive.

Marco opened the bathroom door. Cameron shifted his weight so he could pivot around.

"Don't you touch me, you bastard!" The yell came from inside the bathroom.

Sophia?

Cameron was already in the process of pivoting, so he kept going around to face the other men. But instead of striking them as he had planned, Cameron just glared at Fin.

Fin had his knife up and had obviously been ready for Cameron's attack. There was no way Cameron would've lived through it.

"Okay, maybe I put her in the bathroom, not the closet. So sue me." Cameron shrugged. "Now can we get some coffee?"

The other three men mumbled something to each other and turned to walk out of Cam's room. He heard Marco mutter, "See, I told you." But he didn't hear any response.

Cameron bent down next to Sophia.

"Are you okay? Why are you back? How did you even get in here?" Cameron shot off the questions, knowing he wasn't giving Sophia enough time to respond. There wasn't any time to give her.

Sophia pointed at the window above the bathtub. Cameron couldn't believe, even as slight as Sophia was, that she'd managed to make it through that tiny opening.

He reached down to help her up and heard Sophia's indrawn breath and immediately released her. He noticed the gash on her shoulder.

"What happened?"

"I cut it on my way in through the window. It's not too bad, I think."

"Stay in here. I've got to get to the kitchen and see what's going on. I'll bring back something to wrap your arm with."

Cameron didn't mention that the danger to the operation, and especially Sophia, was more severe now than ever. Unless Cameron could find a way to talk Fin into taking Sophia with them to Mr. Smith's mountain house, things were still going to get ugly real quick. He grabbed his weapon on the way out of the room.

When Cameron arrived in the kitchen, Fin and the other men were sitting around the table. Marco and Rick ate some sort of sugary cereal. Fin was drinking coffee.

Cameron went over to the cabinet, grabbed a mug for coffee, then turned so he was facing the table with his back against the counter.

"So, what the hell, Fin? After all this time you think I'm some sort of cop?"

"Not me, Cam. Sorry, man. It's Smith. He didn't like the whole situation with the woman and told us to make sure everything was under control."

Cameron should've known Smith was the one closer to

figuring things out. Fin and his goons weren't known for their mental prowess.

"We'll have to get rid of her," Fin told Cameron calmly, taking a sip of his coffee as if he wasn't talking about murdering an innocent woman. Next to Fin, Rick looked gleeful at the thought of violence.

A plan came to Cameron—it was a Hail Mary, but it was worth a shot. He didn't like the thought of dragging Sophia in deeper, but at least this would mean not having to end his undercover operation without ever meeting Smith. He was so close.

Cameron thought of his partner, Jason, who had been killed by Smith's order. That made the decision for him. Cameron silently took a deep breath. He was placing all his chips on this one bet.

"Yeah, about getting rid of her." Cameron forced himself to remain casual against the cabinet. "I'm not sure that's the right thing to do."

Rick snickered, but Cameron ignored him. Rick was just upset at the thought of the loss of need for violence.

"Why's that?" Fin asked.

"Well, it ends up that she wasn't in that warehouse by accident yesterday." Now Cameron had everyone's attention. "It ends up that she was there to try to meet and talk to one of us—someone who could get her a meeting with Mr. Smith."

"That's not going to happen," Fin spluttered, obviously thrown. "Mr. Smith doesn't meet with people he doesn't know for no reason."

"Basically that's what I told her," Cameron continued. "I mean, hell, I've known you guys for a long time and I've still never met Mr. Smith."

Fin stood up. "Fine. Then it's settled. Plan still doesn't change."

"Yeah, no problem." Here it went, the Hail Mary. "Oh, yeah, she mentioned knowing something important about a Ghost Rock or something. I have no idea what that is."

Fin froze exactly where he stood, staring at Cameron. Finally he turned and pointed at Rick and Marco. "You two, out. Now." They left their cereal and headed out the door without a word. Fin turned back to Cameron.

"You mean Ghost Shell?" Fin asked slowly.

"Yeah, Ghost Shell. That's it. Not Ghost Rock."

"That woman in your room knows about Ghost Shell?"

"Yeah." Cameron shrugged and took a sip of his coffee, pretending not to notice how completely wound up Fin was. "She said she came to the warehouse so she could find someone who knew Smith and could get her a meeting with him. But then things got out of hand before she could make her play... Guess that's my bad."

Cameron could see the wheels turning in Fin's head, so he continued, "Evidently there's some problem with this Ghost Shell whatever and she knows about it and how to fix it. But she says she'll only talk directly to Smith."

"So make her tell us and we'll tell him."

Cameron shrugged. "She said it can only be shown with the Ghost Shell. Whatever that is. She said Mr. Smith would be very glad to have the information."

Fin began pacing back and forth. "Mr. Smith isn't available today. I can't get in touch with him at all."

Cameron breathed a sigh of relief. Dealing with just Fin was much easier than dealing with Mr. Smith, someone Cameron didn't know at all. "Well, it's totally up to you, Fin. You know best. But I say, what harm can there be in bringing her? We can get rid of her there just as easily as here, if Mr. Smith doesn't want her around."

Cameron could see Fin considering the idea. Obviously the man was not supposed to bring unvetted strangers to meet Smith. But if that stranger was useful… "You could save the day, Fin. Whatever Ghost Shell is, it's obviously important to Mr. Smith. If this woman knows something helpful, you could be a real hero."

The thought of being in Smith's good graces was obviously the little push Fin needed. "All right, fine, we'll take her with us to the mountain house. But she's your responsibility. And you're the one going down if she doesn't have the info she says she does."

"That's cool, man. I think she does, though. She seems really smart."

"Oh, yeah?" Finn scoffed. "When did you guys have a little heart-to-heart talk?"

"Whoa, nothing like that." Cameron laughed good-naturedly. "Just after we had our…fun, she brought it up."

"Yeah?" Suspicion came back into Fin's eyes. "Was that before or after she hit you in the head?"

Cameron thought fast. "What can I say? We both like it rough. She obviously can give as good as she gets. We're beginning to grow on each other."

Evidently that was enough to satisfy Fin. "Whatever. Just have her and yourself ready to go soon. We'll be leaving in a couple of hours." With that, Fin turned and headed out of the kitchen.

Cameron took a sip of his coffee, but found it had gone cold so he dumped it in the sink. His plan had worked. Sophia was safe. His undercover operation was still intact and he was going to meet Smith. Cameron was one step closer to bringing that bastard down, acquiring Ghost Shell and getting Sophia to safety in one piece.

But the dread pooling in his stomach told him the opposite was true.

Chapter Eight

A few hours later Cameron watched out the jet window over Sophia's shoulder as they came in for their landing in the Blue Ridge Mountains area of western Virginia. There was nothing around but trees for miles in any direction. The airstrip they landed at was tiny, similar to the small airport south of Washington, DC, they'd taken off from not too long before. Neither was being monitored by anyone who didn't work for DS-13, Cameron was sure.

Cameron looked over at Sophia, who stared blankly out the window. Dark circles of exhaustion, almost like bruises, ringed her eyes. She held his hand in a death grip.

After convincing Fin to take Sophia with them to meet Smith, Cameron had made his way back to his room. Sophia had still been sitting on the bathroom floor, almost in a daze, arm still bleeding. He'd cleaned the cut and wrapped it with gauze. It didn't look as if it needed stitches, but it still wasn't pretty.

He still didn't know exactly why she had done it, but her return had saved his life, without a doubt.

"Thank you," Cameron had whispered when he was finished with her wound, putting his hands reverently on either side of her face and kissing her gently.

Sophia had just nodded.

Since coming back into DS-13's grasp, Sophia had

hardly said one word to Cameron, although he had to admit, talking had been nearly impossible. By the time he had played out his wounded-because-you-don't-trust-me part for Fin and the gang, and gotten suitable apologies, it had almost been time to go.

Cameron found a shirt for Sophia to wear—hers had lost all the buttons, much to the delight of the DS-13 men. He had wanted to talk to Sophia about what had happened, but sending an encoded message to Omega Sector with his satellite phone had been more important. He had to let Omega Sector know they were moving—to an unknown location as of yet—and that there was now an innocent third party involved. Cameron would send more info when he had time and details.

As the plane came to a halt, everybody unbuckled their seat belts and stood. Except Sophia. She still stared vacantly out the window.

Fin opened the plane door and everyone began to file out. When Sophia still didn't move, Cameron squatted down in front of her. He took her hands, which lay limply in her lap, in his.

"Hey," he whispered. He watched as her eyes, shadowed with exhaustion, turned blankly toward him. "You doing okay?"

Sophia nodded slowly. "Where are we?"

"We're in the mountains. Going to the evil lair, remember?"

The ghost of a smile crossed her lips. "They don't call it an evil lair."

Cameron winked at her and rubbed the back of both of her hands with his thumbs. They were like ice. "That's right, sweetie. You going to be all right? I know this is really hard."

Sophia nodded again. "I just don't know what to do,

Cam." She leaned in closer to him and whispered urgently, "I know I work for the Bureau, but I'm an artist! I don't have any training. I don't know anything about working… you know, in situations like this."

Cameron unbuckled her seat belt and helped Sophia stand. "Just stay as close to me as possible, and try to ignore everyone else. Can you do that?"

Sophia gave a short bark of near-hysterical laughter. "Uh, yeah. No problem wanting to stay away from them. Especially that Rick guy—he freaks me out."

Cameron knew Rick had a cruel, violent streak. He didn't blame Sophia for wanting to stay away. "All right, let's go." Cameron quickly sent out the coordinates of this landing strip in a message to Omega Sector—a risky move, but one he had to make. Then he led Sophia down the few short steps of the small plane and over to the SUV that was waiting just off the runway. He got in the backseat with Sophia, noticing how she avoided looking at anyone.

And how every man in the vehicle looked at her. Cameron would have to keep Sophia with him as much as possible. She was definitely not safe alone.

Cameron paid very close attention as they drove from the airstrip to the mountain house. If for some reason he was not able to get GPS coordinates to Omega Sector, he would have to rely on his own observation and memory to find the "evil lair" again. They were headed northwest on a pretty steady incline. Mr. Smith's hideout must be near the top of one of these mountains. The Blue Ridge Mountains of Virginia weren't tall and barren like the Rockies. There were little peaks of hills everywhere, where homes could be built and privacy abounded.

Many of these homes had one way in, and one way out. Which was obviously the case here, Cameron realized. There hadn't been a single turnoff or other car on the road since they'd left the airstrip. Smart move on Mr. Smith's part.

Cameron hated that Sophia was here, but was excited that he was finally making such strong headway in the case. Today, finally—*finally*—he was going to meet Mr. Smith. Cameron knew he couldn't arrest Smith right away, he'd definitely need Omega Sector backup first. Plus, acquiring Ghost Shell took precedence over any arrest, but he couldn't help but feel hopeful that he was going to be able to do both.

Cameron glanced over at Sophia, who was staring blankly out the window again. He just hoped she could keep it together. He reached over and took her hand, subtly, so nobody else in the car could see. She looked over at him.

She could obviously recognize his concern. She nodded slightly and gave an attempt at a smile. Cameron squeezed her hand, wishing he could do more.

After just a few more minutes the car started making an even steeper incline. It wasn't long before they were at the DS-13 mountain house, or evil lair, or whatever you wanted to call it.

It definitely was no jackass-infested rat hole. Well, maybe it was jackass-infested, but it certainly wasn't a rat hole. The house was gorgeous and huge—a surprisingly tasteful blend of wood and large stone. Giant windows made up huge sections of walls, providing unobstructed views of the spectacular hills of the Blue Ridge Mountains.

And unobstructed views of anyone who might be trying to get up to the house through those hills. Any sort of covert attack of any magnitude would be nearly impossible. Definitely something Cameron would have to communicate to Omega Sector, if they planned to take down Mr. Smith here.

The beauty of the building and the surroundings were

breathtaking, but Cameron forced himself to stay focused solely on the job at hand. The SUV pulled into a four-car garage that attached to the house through a walkway.

They all got out of the vehicle, grabbed their bags and made their way inside. Sophia stayed almost glued to Cameron's side, clutching his arm. Rick was quick to comment on it.

"Seems like someone is a little friendlier this morning, Cam."

Cameron smirked at him. "Yeah, well, I guess I'm just that charming."

Rick smirked back. "Maybe you should give me a chance to be charming with her. I'm a pretty charming guy." Rick took a step toward Sophia. Cameron immediately felt Sophia's grip on his arm tighten.

"Not going to happen, Rick. So just run along." Cameron shooed him away. Anger flared in the other man's eyes, but he said nothing.

Cameron gave a short whistle as they walked into the house. It was even more impressive on the inside than it was on the outside. "Wow, this is quite a place," Cameron told Fin as he looked around.

Fin nodded, grinning. "Ten bedrooms. Eleven baths. Half a dozen offices and meeting rooms. A formal dining room and even a party area. Try not to get lost."

A man who was probably a member of DS-13, but looked like a butler, came through a doorway from the back and started walking toward them. Tension filled Fin and the other goons at the man's presence. As subtly as he could, Cameron put himself between Sophia and this unknown person.

There were too many damn unknowns in this situation.

The man obviously knew Fin, but spoke with a formal tone. "Mr. Fin, welcome. As you know, your uncle will be arriving later this evening, bringing some other guests for a weekend soiree."

Fin fidgeted. "Um, yeah, Thompson, thanks. My uncle told me about the party. This is Cam Cameron. Cam, this is Thompson."

Thompson nodded. "Yes, Mr. Smith mentioned his arrival. And Mr. Cameron's guest? She was not mentioned."

Fin looked uncomfortable. "Yeah. She's with Cam. Has some information for Mr. Smith that we think he'll be very happy to hear." Fin lifted his chin in an attempt to look confident.

"I will show you to your room, Mr. Cameron, and your guest, also." Thompson turned to Cameron. "Everyone else has been here before and is familiar with the house."

"Good, because I'm tired as hell since I had to spend most of the night convincing everyone I'm not a liar." Cameron gave a dramatic sigh. He picked up his duffel from where he had set it on the floor and began following Thompson, the butler guy.

"Uncle?" Cameron said with an eyebrow raised as he passed Fin. "Who's the lying SOB now?"

Fin just laughed and shrugged and headed off to another part of the house.

Thompson led Cameron down the hall with Sophia following close behind, still holding his hand. Every once in a while he could feel a shudder run through her. She was swaying on her feet and Cameron knew he needed to get her to the room soon. He breathed a sigh of relief when the older man opened a door for them.

Cameron ushered Sophia inside, then turned to their escort. "Thanks, man. We're just going to crash for a while," Cameron told him while shutting the door in his face.

Cameron locked the door and looked around the room. It was definitely much nicer than the DS-13 house in DC.

A huge four-poster bed, made of the same wood as the rest of the house, dominated much of the room. There was a dresser against one wall and two sitting chairs over by the massive sliding glass doors that led out to a small deck.

There were two doors over on the far wall. Cameron walked over to them. One was a closet. He quickly closed the door, praying they wouldn't need to use it. The other door led to a bathroom. Cameron whistled as he took in the huge hot tub and separate shower. This whole place was gorgeous and tasteful.

Cameron walked back into the bedroom and saw that Sophia had wandered over to the windows and was staring out vacantly, just as she had on the plane. He wanted to talk to her, but first he needed to check that their room wasn't bugged.

Cameron took what would look like a smartphone to any casual observer and punched in a code. This turned on a scanner that allowed him to see if there were any electronic transmissions being sent from anywhere in the room. It wasn't a foolproof way of checking for surveillance, but it was pretty useful.

There were no transmissions being sent from anywhere in this room. Not surprising. Criminals rarely recorded what was going on in their own homes if they were smart. Too many ways for it to be used against them.

Cameron walked over to Sophia and put his hands on her shoulders, then looked out at the view with her.

"Beautiful, isn't it?" she asked softly.

"Breathtaking. I wish we were here under different circumstances." He pulled her back against his chest and was relieved when she didn't pull away.

Sophia nodded. "Me, too."

Cameron turned her around so he could see her face.

"Soph, why did you come back? Don't get me wrong, I'm thankful that you did. But *why*?"

Sophia looked around the room. "Is it okay to talk here?"

"Yeah, I checked for bugs. The room's clean."

"I was on my way out and I heard Rick and that other guy talking. Fin still didn't trust you completely. I was the final test for you."

Cameron felt himself tense. He'd had no idea. Fin—on Mr. Smith's orders—had set him up, and Cameron had been oblivious.

"You saved my life," Cameron whispered.

Sophia just smiled and shrugged. "So I guess we're even."

Cameron saw Sophia wince at the shrug. "Is your shoulder okay?"

She nodded. "Yes, just stiff. How's your head?"

Cameron winced but grinned. "You've got a pretty mean swing there, Miss Reardon."

"I'm sorry I'm still here, Cam. I know I complicate everything."

Cameron trailed a finger down her cheek. "Well, if you weren't here, I'd probably be dead. So I'm pretty damn glad you're here."

Sophia swayed on her feet. Cameron caught her quickly before she fell and led her over to the bed.

"You need to sleep," he told her gently as he pulled the covers back on the giant bed and ushered her in.

Sophia didn't say anything, just slipped her shoes off and lay down, fully clothed. She was asleep before he could pull the covers over her.

Cameron slipped his own shoes off and walked around to the other side of the bed. He slipped under the covers next to Sophia.

She was right; her presence here did complicate everything. But hell, Sophia complicated his life just by breathing. He reached over and pulled her sleeping body into his arms.

Cameron didn't have a plan, and that made him nervous. If it was just his life on the line then he'd be willing to fly blind as long as possible if it meant his goal was accomplished.

He kissed the top of Sophia's head as she snuggled in closer to him. Not having a plan when it was Sophia in jeopardy was unacceptable to him. So he would need to come up with one. Fast.

WHEN SOPHIA OPENED her eyes again the sun was setting. She sat straight up as she tried to remember where she was and who she was with. And then it all came back to her.

She knew Cameron had slept with her in the bed. She remembered waking up in a panic and finding him right by her side, rubbing her back and easing her to lie back down on the bed.

She could tell he had been there next to her until recently. The pillow still held the indentation from his head. She didn't know if he had slept this whole time with her or not, but she was thankful he had been there, next to her. She touched the place where Cameron had lain.

Sophia laid back in the luxurious bed now and stretched. No matter what, this place was definitely nicer than the rat hole they'd been in yesterday. But somehow that didn't make Sophia feel much better.

She turned over to her side and saw Cameron staring out the window. He seemed deep in thought. He was wearing only his jeans and his arms were crossed over his naked chest. He was definitely more muscular than when Sophia had last seen him five years ago. He had been fit then, but now the muscles in his chest, back and arms were even more pronounced.

And that six-pack he had acquired was definitely mouth-watering. Sophia once again wished they were here under different circumstances. That there wasn't so much weight riding on his shoulders, even if they seemed broad enough to carry anything.

Sophia got out of the bed and wandered over to stand next to Cameron. "Hey," she whispered.

"Feeling better?" he asked.

"Yeah. It's amazing what a few hours of sleep can do."

"You definitely needed it. I don't know how you were holding it together." They stood in companionable silence for a few moments, looking out the window. Sophia wanted to wrap an arm around Cameron, but wasn't sure if it would be appropriate. Or welcome.

"So do we have a plan? What do I need to do?"

Cameron turned so they were looking face-to-face at each other. "I've been thinking a lot while you were asleep. I have a plan." He didn't look too thrilled with it, though.

"Hopefully a better one than me running down this mountain in the middle of the night by myself?" Sophia joked, but inside she was afraid that was what she was going to have to do.

"No, you won't have to run all the way down. I'll have an extraction team waiting."

Sophia shook her head. "Last time I *escaped*, it almost got you killed. What makes you think it's a good plan this time?"

"It won't be just you. We'll both be going."

"I don't understand. How will that work? What about this case?"

Cameron didn't answer.

Sophia wasn't sure she was understanding exactly what

was going on here. "But what about all your work? The eight months with DS-13? The weeks in the jackass-infested rat hole?"

Cameron turned to the side and looked back out the window. He shrugged.

"You can't do this, Cameron. What about the justice for your partner?"

Sophia watched as Cameron took a deep breath and ran his hand through his thick, dark hair. "Soph, I watched you there while you were sleeping. You're covered in bruises. You have a huge, nasty cut on your shoulder."

"But—" Sophia tried to cut in but he wouldn't let her. He turned and held both of her arms in his hands, careful not to put any pressure on her wound.

"No, listen. You've been absolutely amazing. You've kept your head and you've kept it together, when you had every reason to fall apart." He brought her a little closer. "And then, when you had a chance to get away, you came back for me, Soph. You saved my life."

Sophia just shrugged. There hadn't been any option for her. She wasn't going to leave him there to die.

"I want justice so bad for my partner that I can taste it, Soph. And there's other stuff, too, that you don't even know about. But that will all have to be taken care of another way at another time. I'm not going to risk your life. I'm going to call in for help and we're getting out of here tonight."

A sudden vibration from a small cell-phone-looking thing on the nightstand by the bed caught both of their attentions. Cameron quickly walked over and grabbed it. Sophia watched as Cameron twisted the box inside out and began typing a series of symbols on it. Then he stopped and waited, saying nothing. A few moments later the inside-out box beeped.

This time Cameron brought it up to his ear and spoke into it. "Omega, go. Code 44802. Security confirmed."

Cameron listened for a few moments to whatever was being said on the other end.

"Coordinates are confirmed. Primary target has not arrived."

Whatever was being said to Cameron did not make him happy. "Roger that. Secondary target has not arrived, then. Primary target location has not been ascertained."

More talk from the other end.

"Request withdrawal assistance tonight."

Now whatever was being said was really making Cameron mad.

"Bystander in pocket, but too many unknowns. Immediate assistance requested."

Cameron turned and looked directly at Sophia while he listened. She could see his teeth grit and a vein flicker at his neck. "No, there is no immediate threat to bystander. But again I repeat—there are too many unknowns."

Sophia watched as Cameron's fist clenched at his side.

"Roger that. Primary objective understood."

Cameron poked a series of buttons angrily into the phone. He turned it inside out so it just looked like a regular phone again and placed it on the nightstand again.

Sophia wasn't completely sure what she had just heard, but it sounded as if they were completely on their own.

Chapter Nine

Cameron wanted to throw the satellite phone across the room, but knew it wouldn't do any good. He drew a breath and released it, trying to focus. Being angry at Omega Sector's unwillingness to send a rescue team in immediately was not going to help anything. He needed to work the problem.

And right now the problem was standing a few feet away from him, engulfed by his T-shirt, with tousled brown hair and gorgeous green eyes.

He couldn't get her out. Cameron had to face that. She was watching him with intent eyes, looking so tiny. But she was far from helpless. Sophia wasn't a trained agent—as she was so quick to point out—but she was smart, and quick-thinking.

Cameron wanted Sophia out of there. But according to Omega Sector that wasn't an option. So she was about to become his partner.

Cameron stretched his arm out to Sophia and she walked hesitantly to him, questions in her eyes.

"Moving to plan B?" she asked. "No backup from the Bureau?"

Cameron nodded. "Yeah." He hesitated. "Except I don't work for the Bureau."

Sophia took a step back. "You don't?" Cameron could

see her trying to figure out who he was working undercover for if it wasn't the FBI. "Are you DEA? Some sort of local law enforcement?"

"No. I'm part of what's called Omega Sector. We're an interagency task force. All the advantages of having the resources of individual agencies—DEA, FBI, Marshals Service, ATF, hell, even INTERPOL sometimes. But much less red tape."

"So basically you're like your own Justice League."

Cameron smiled at the Saturday-morning cartoon reference. "Yeah, basically. But without superpowers."

"I've worked at the Bureau for four years now. I've never heard of Omega Sector."

"No, you wouldn't have. It's not something you can just apply for. You're recruited by Omega, or you don't get in at all. They're looking for specific skills, mind-sets, abilities."

Sophia took another small step away from Cameron, frowning. "And you had all those things."

Cameron shrugged. "I guess so."

"How long has Omega Sector been around?"

"About ten years."

"And when did you begin working for them?"

Cameron grimaced. There was no way around this. "Five years ago."

Sophia's head snapped up and Cameron could see realization dawn in her eyes. Omega Sector was the reason he had never said goodbye to her.

Sophia turned and walked over to the window. Cameron stayed where he was over by the bed, giving her space.

"So they recruited you?"

"Yes."

Sophia continued to look out the window. "I'm not surprised. You're obviously good at this sort of thing."

"I wanted to make a difference in the world, Soph. Omega Sector was that chance."

Sophia nodded, still not looking at him. "And I suppose because it's all top secret and stuff, you couldn't tell anybody."

"Sophia…"

"You know what? I don't even want to talk about this right now. You wanted to make a difference. You joined your *Super Friends* group and have been doing that ever since. Congratulations."

Her back and shoulders were ramrod-straight as she stared out the window. What she didn't say stood like a giant between them.

You wanted to make a difference more than you wanted to be with me.

Cameron was glad she didn't say it out loud, because he had no idea how he would respond. Yes, he had wanted to fight bad guys when he had joined Omega Sector five years ago. And at the time, it had been the most important thing in the world to him. He and Sophia had been at the beginning of their relationship. No promises, no real commitment. They hadn't even slept together.

Casual. At least that's what Cameron had told himself. But he had known they both were taking it seriously. Every morning when he had met her at the little diner for breakfast, he had known they weren't casual.

And with five years of perspective, Cameron could see exactly what he had given up. Having Sophia standing here right in front of him, and having no way of getting her out of the danger, made him think perhaps it wasn't worth it after all.

After a moment, Sophia turned to Cameron. "So Omega Sector deems arresting Mr. Smith more important than getting us out? I mean, I can understand you wanting to get him because of your partner. But if you've decided to cut out? It sounds like you maybe just moved from one jackass-infested place to another."

Cameron gave her a half smile. "Actually, I haven't told you everything."

Sophia closed her eyes briefly and shook her head. "Of course you haven't. What's new?"

"Arresting anybody in DS-13 has become secondary in this op. Instead, it's something in his possession that Omega Sector has deemed more important than either of our individual lives. And they're probably right to feel that way."

Now Cameron had Sophia's attention. "What is it?"

Cameron explained to her the details of Ghost Shell. How, if used by terrorists, it could cripple computer and communication equipment of law enforcement and first responders, basically by using their own communication equipment against them.

"They'd be pretty paralyzed against any sort of terrorist attack or anything like that," Sophia whispered after Cameron finished explaining.

"Yes." Cameron walked over to her at the window. "It's not an actual weapon, but in some ways this technology is more devastating than any one weapon. Law enforcement's reliance on computers and communication technology is pretty heavy."

Sophia nodded. "How did Omega Sector find out about it?"

"I'm not sure exactly. Somebody, evidently a law-abiding computer scientist person, who had been working on something similar, reported it and the report made its way to Omega Sector."

"And they found out DS-13 has it?"

"Yes. But DS-13 isn't interested in using it against law enforcement. They don't have any political or religious ambitions—they're only interested in money. They want to sell it on the black market. Absolute chaos, available to the highest bidder."

"Oh, my gosh, Cam. In the wrong hands..." Sophia shook her head.

"I know. So like I said, I can understand why Omega Sector said no to us getting out. But I don't like it."

Neither of them said anything for a few moments. Sophia turned and took a step toward him.

"Is the Ghost Shell drive here?" she whispered finally.

"If not right now, then definitely soon, when Smith arrives. Although I don't know exactly where. Omega is afraid if they come in here full force, someone from DS-13 could escape with Ghost Shell."

She looked up at him, having to crane her neck to do so. God, she was so tiny. "Then we'll find it. And we'll get out of here," she said.

Cameron framed her face with his hands. "Soph, I can't ask you to risk your life like that. They killed my partner because they found out he was undercover. They won't hesitate to kill us, too."

"No offense, Cam, but my life is already in jeopardy. I might as well do something useful."

Cameron shook his head. He didn't like it; Sophia in the line of fire was definitely not his first choice. But it didn't look as if he had any choice at all.

Unbelievably, Sophia smiled at him. "You know, when I interviewed for my job as a graphic artist for the FBI four years ago, one of the first things I asked my boss was if I would ever be in life-threatening situations. I was assured I wouldn't be."

Cameron chuckled softly. "You mean they didn't list this situation in your job description? Hard to believe."

Sophia took a step back from Cameron. "I'll try not to

get in your way, but I'm definitely not cut out for secret-agent spy stuff." She shrugged and used her hair to hide her face. "I'm hardly capable of walking inside my own closet to pick out clothes without having a panic attack, much less do anything courageous."

"Hey." Cameron tucked her brown hair back behind her ear. "Don't talk that way. You've done a damn good job so far."

Sophia just shrugged again. "I'm going to take a shower. I feel like I've got grime under my grime," she told Cameron. He didn't stop her from pulling away.

"You might want to take a soak in the tub. It's huge."

Sophia sighed. A soak in a tub sounded like the most wonderful thing she had ever heard in her entire life. "That's definitely where I'll be."

"Okay." Cameron smiled at her. "Then we'll go find something to eat. I'm starving."

"Me, too."

Cameron watched as Sophia made her way to the bathroom and closed the door behind her.

He could hear the water running from her bath, and tried to think of every possible other thing in the world except Sophia naked behind that bathroom door.

Cameron wasn't sure he'd ever found a task so difficult in his entire life.

A sharp rap on the room's other door drew Cameron's attention. He quickly pulled his shirt over his head and grabbed his SIG from the nightstand.

"Yeah?" he asked from the door without opening it.

"It's Thompson, Mr. Cameron. I've got some food for you and Ms. Reardon."

Thompson knew Sophia's name. Cameron wasn't sure if that was good or bad. He needed to be prepared for either.

Cameron opened the door and Thompson walked in with

a tray of food. Thank God Sophia was in the bathroom, out of sight and earshot.

"Thanks, man." Cameron was once again struck by how much Thompson looked and acted like a butler. But he could see how lightly the man moved on his feet and how perfectly balanced he was when carrying the tray and setting it down.

Cameron had no doubt that Thompson was much more than just a butler. The suspicion was confirmed when he saw the older man glance around the room subtly, taking in all details.

This man, more than any of the goons Cameron had hung out with in DS-13 for the past eight months, was dangerous. No doubt that was why Mr. Smith kept him around.

"Something I can help you find?" Cameron asked.

Thompson looked at Cameron and tipped his head slightly, as if respecting that he had been caught snooping, but not apologizing for it.

"Will Ms. Reardon be requiring anything?" Thompson asked as he set the tray of food on a small table by the closet.

Cameron did not want to talk about Sophia with this man. "No, she's fine."

Cameron answered a little too quickly. He cursed silently as he saw that Thompson realized it, too. The last thing he wanted to do was show DS-13, especially this man whom Cameron was beginning to suspect was much higher up in the food chain than he had thought, that he cared about Sophia. They wouldn't hesitate to use her against him.

Cameron wandered nonchalantly over to the food. He picked up an apple and took a big bite.

"I can take care of her just fine, if you know what I mean." Cameron gave the man a wink. "She's in the bathroom relaxing in that swimming pool you call a tub. Working out the kinks."

Cameron saw Thompson's eyes narrow in distaste before the man hid his response. Good. Better for Cameron to seem crude and obnoxious than as if he had some sort of attachment to Sophia.

"Mr. Smith and his other guests have arrived. Mr. Smith would like to meet with you and Ms. Reardon in one hour."

Cameron took another bite of his apple. "That's cool, man. Whatever." And because it seemed to make Thompson so uncomfortable before, Cameron winked at him again.

"Yes, well, good. Until then, please stay in your room and keep Ms. Reardon here with you."

Thompson turned and made his way out of the room quickly and efficiently.

Cameron looked over at the elaborate tray of food Thompson had brought in. Fruits, cheeses, meats and breads for sandwiches. Quite the spread. All laid out on a large silver platter with oversize handles.

Cameron began moving the food, piece by piece, off the tray. Based on what he had observed about Thompson, Cameron was willing to bet there was some sort of surveillance device somewhere on this tray. Once all the food was off the tray and he was able to turn it over, he saw a transmitter. But something about how large it was and how it sat in the handle was a little too obvious to Cameron.

Sure enough, Cameron kept searching and found it a couple minutes later: a tiny transmitter under the lip of the least descriptive part of the tray, where you would hardly think to look, especially if you found the first device.

Sneaky little bastard.

Thompson had almost caught them unawares. Cameron decided to leave the transmitting device where it was, fully functional, since it was sound-only. He and Sophia could use it to their advantage. But the larger, more obvious device, Cameron removed.

"Screw you, Thompson, and whoever else is listening. I prefer not to have an audience, you perverts," Cameron said into the piece of equipment. He then threw the transmitter on the ground and stomped on it.

So now they thought he had no idea they were listening. Good, he had no problem exploiting their overconfidence.

SOPHIA FELT LIKE a new person after her long soak in the tub. She had to put the same clothes back on, so that wasn't great, but at least her muscles were easing. Somehow being taken hostage by a crime syndicate group tended to make you tense and tight. Go figure.

Sophia came out of the door, her head wrapped in a towel, ready to boast to Cameron about the miracles of a hot tub. "Hey, seriously, it's almost like we're on a…"

She was cut off by him pushing her back against the wall and kissing her. Thoroughly.

Her arms, almost of their own accord, traveled up his arms to his shoulders. The towel around her hair came loose then slipped from her head and fell to the floor. Sophia forgot everything but the heat and strength of the kiss.

She stood up on her tiptoes to get closer and wound her fingers in his hair. She didn't care where they were anymore or the danger they were facing. She wanted Cameron now and he wanted her. That was all that mattered.

Cameron's lips moved over her jaw and up to Sophia's ear. She shivered with every light kiss he placed. His hands grasped her waist and pulled her closer to him. Sophia found herself melting into him.

"They're listening to everything we say," he murmured almost silently against her ear.

It took a moment for the words to penetrate. Sophia's arms fell to her sides. Cold washed over her where moments ago there had been such heat.

Cameron wasn't kissing her because he wanted to. He was kissing her to keep her quiet. It was just as effective as the backhand at the warehouse. And just as painful.

Sophia nodded jerkily. Cameron tried to kiss her again, but she turned her head away. There was no need to kiss her—she got the message: don't say or do anything stupid.

Or maybe do anything *more* stupid than throw herself into a kiss that meant nothing to the other person.

Sophia nodded again and reached down to get the towel that had fallen from her head. She was so cold. And she needed to be away from Cameron. Immediately.

"That's a big tub they have in there." Sophia didn't recognize her own voice as she said it, wasn't even sure how she got the words out of her mouth.

Thankfully Cameron stepped away from her.

"There's some food over on the table, if you're hungry. Thompson brought it while you were in the bathroom." Cameron pointed toward the table.

So that's how they could hear now but couldn't before— something on the tray. Sophia nodded, not quite making eye contact with Cameron—she couldn't stand to do that yet, not after the fool she'd just made of herself—and went to the table.

Although she'd totally lost her appetite, Sophia forced herself to eat. She chewed bite after tasteless bite, forcing the needed nutrients into her system.

But damn it, she felt like an idiot. Cameron was undercover. She needed to get that through her evidently very thick skull. Arresting this Mr. Smith guy and getting back Ghost Shell were the most important things to him.

And her safety, she had to give him that, too. But he

was undercover; nothing he said or did should be taken at face value.

"I'm glad you liked the tub," Cameron finally said from across the room.

"Yeah, I could definitely get used to that sort of luxury," Sophia responded. Cameron nodded encouragingly and spun his finger in a circle, gesturing for her to continue that line of conversation.

"Someday I want to own a giant tub like that one," Sophia continued as she ate another bite of a sandwich from the tray.

Cameron started talking, making up a crazy story about a hot tub he had once snuck into with his brothers while in high school and the shenanigans that ensued. At least Sophia *thought* he was making it up. She knew Cameron had two brothers and a sister, so maybe it was true.

Without ever missing a beat with his story, Cameron walked over to Sophia and led her away from the tray to over near the bed. He let out a loud guffaw as he finished the story and Sophia laughed along with him.

"Soph," he said in a low voice that wasn't quite a whisper, pulling her closer. "Smith is here. Ghost Shell is probably with him."

"Okay. That's good, right?" she whispered.

"Don't whisper," he told her in that same low tone. "Just speak very low, if you don't want them to hear. Whispers are actually easier for surveillance equipment to pick up than very low tones."

Sophia nodded.

Cameron brought his voice back up to normal range. "Mr. Smith wants to meet us in an hour. So it's probably good that you went ahead and took a bath already."

Cameron looked at Sophia, gesturing with his head that she should say something. "O-okay..." she said tentatively.

Cameron leaned closer, dropping his voice so the surveillance couldn't hear. "Remember, you want this meeting. That's how I convinced Fin to let you come here, by telling him you had information to give to Smith."

Sophia nodded. "Yeah, good." She said in a louder voice, "That's what I'm here for, to meet Smith. I just want to make this exchange and get out of here."

Cameron nodded with enthusiasm.

"I don't like the mountains," she continued. "I'm more of a beach person." That was totally not true, but seemed like a reasonable thing to say.

"Yeah, me, too," Cameron said. "Why don't we go on a little vacation after all this?"

Sophia had to remind herself that Cameron wasn't really talking to her; this was just part of his undercover story. She refused to allow herself to wish he wanted to spend time with her. When this was finished, he'd be gone again, just like five years ago.

"Yeah, sure." There was decidedly less enthusiasm in her tone.

Cameron's head cocked to the side as he studied Sophia with questioning eyes. She didn't dare explain to him what was really bothering her, even if there wasn't a bug in the room.

A knock on the door saved the moment. She saw Cameron reach for the gun he evidently had tucked in the back of his jeans. He walked silently to the door, gesturing for her to move back toward the bathroom.

"Yes?" he asked without opening the door.

Something was murmured that Sophia couldn't quite catch, but whatever it was caused Cameron to relax and put his gun away. He opened the door, and someone handed him a package.

"Here, this is for you." Cameron tossed the box onto the bed.

Sophia frowned and walked over to it. Pushing the tissue paper to the side she found clothes: a pair of stylishly cut black pants, and a soft gray sweater. Undergarments, socks and shoes completed the outfit. All of them were the perfect size for her.

Sophia looked up at Cameron. "What? Where did this come from?"

Cameron pointed over at the tray to remind her they were being listened to. "Beats me. I didn't have anything to do with it. But I guess you couldn't meet Mr. Smith in my T-shirt, now could you? So it's a good thing."

"Yeah, I guess so." Sophia turned toward the bathroom, more disturbed than she cared to admit. Did Smith just keep women's clothes sitting around? Probably not. Which meant someone with a very good eye had taken her measurements and gotten clothes up to this remote location pretty darn quickly.

Somehow the arrival of these clothes, more than any of the other things—much more dangerous things—that had happened to her over the past two days, made it hit home the power of the people Cameron was dealing with. They had resources. They had manpower. And they had a scary attention to detail.

Plus, they were murderers.

As Cameron came into the bathroom with her and started providing details about Ghost Shell in a hushed tone, Sophia clutched the box of clothes to her chest and listened as best she could. When Cameron had given her all the info he could, he left, closing the door behind him so Sophia could dress.

She did so, hoping the clothes provided by a murdering crime syndicate wouldn't be the last ones she ever put on.

Chapter Ten

There was no more Cameron could do to prepare Sophia, even though he knew it wasn't enough. Time was up. Eight months undercover had all led up to this.

And it was all out of his hands and completely in Sophia's.

Cameron knew that wasn't quite accurate, but it certainly felt like it as they followed Thompson down an extended hallway of the large house to a set of rooms in the back. By their very location, the rooms were less accessible, discouraging any wandering guests from finding them. Not hidden, exactly, just not advertised. And something about Thompson just kept nagging at Cameron.

Cameron watched Sophia from the corner of his eye as she walked beside him. She was glancing around nervously, as if looking for exits. She rubbed her fists against the legs of her black pants. Cameron wished he could catch her hand and hold it, but knew strolling in like lovers was not the way they should meet Smith.

Cameron looked over at Sophia and smiled. Sophia gnawed on her lip a moment more before taking a deep breath and straightening her shoulders.

"You okay?" Cam whispered.

"Doesn't really make a difference now, does it?" Sophia said without looking at him.

Not exactly the reassuring answer he was hoping for.

Cameron tried to go through multiple possible scenarios in his head. What he would do if Sophia freaked out. How he could help her keep it together. Their best route of escape if they had to run. Weaponless and outnumbered, none of the options were good. Cameron prayed Sophia wouldn't panic. But they were walking into a situation that would make even the most seasoned undercover agent wary. He could only imagine the terror Sophia was feeling.

Again, not reassuring.

Thompson led them to a door at the farthest end of the hallway. Cameron pretended not to watch as the older man used a card to swipe a lock on the wall. Cameron wondered who else might have a key card to this office.

Cameron looked over at Sophia again. She was no longer clenching and unclenching her small fists, so that was good. Thompson opened the door for them and Cameron gestured for Sophia to walk in ahead of him. Showtime.

They walked into the expansive office, Cameron taking in as much as he could about the room without actually looking as if he was. Sophia made no such pretense. Most of the walls were lined with deep cherry bookshelves and cabinetry. The far wall was made up of windows, showcasing the wondrous view of nature outside. A large desk took up the area near the window, with a black luxury office chair behind it. The chair was currently facing the windows, away from the desk.

Slowly the large chair swiveled around so the man in it was facing Cameron and Sophia. There was no doubt this man was related to Fin—his build, facial structure and coloring were all similar, yet he was older and flabbier than Fin. This was it; the moment Cameron had waited over a year for.

"I'm Mr. Smith," the man said in a somewhat squeaky

voice that belied his overweight size. His Yankee accent was thick. His eyes small, close-set, almost beady. "Go ahead and sit down."

Cameron's lips pressed tight and his shoulders slumped as he sat. *This* man was one of the top members of DS-13 and had eluded law enforcement for years? Somehow he just wasn't what Cameron had expected. But perhaps nothing short of an absolute monster would've lived up to Cameron's expectations.

Regardless of whether the man fit the image Cameron had built in his head, Cameron was tempted to arrest him right there, everything else be damned. Omega could figure out another way to get Ghost Shell. Only the thought of Sophia trapped in the middle of all this halted him. Cameron settled back into his seat, clenching his jaw.

Thompson came around to stand next to the desk, close to Smith's side. Out of the corner of his eye Cameron noticed Smith glancing at Thompson and Thompson giving a slight nod. Immediately Cameron was on high alert. Obviously some sort of signal had passed between the two men, but what did it mean? Cameron wished to God that Thompson hadn't done a weapons check back at the room. Cameron felt naked without his SIG. Were he and Sophia about to be assassinated while Cameron was able to do nothing?

But neither Smith nor Thompson made any aggressive moves. Instead, Smith settled back in his chair and Thompson remained watchful and alert where he stood. Maybe Cameron had imagined the entire thing.

Cameron leaned forward in his chair and offered Smith his hand to shake, although he really wanted to break the offending hand. "Mr. Smith, it's a pleasure to finally meet you." Cameron managed not to choke on the words.

"Likewise, Cam," the older man answered as he shook

Cameron's hand with his large sweaty paws. Cameron resisted the urge to wipe his palms on the legs of his pants.

Mr. Smith continued, "I realize you've worked with DS-13 for a long time, Cam, without meeting me. I hope you understand the necessary security precautions." Smith glanced at Thompson again.

"Oh, sure, Mr. Smith. Everybody has to be careful in this day and age." Cameron nodded enthusiastically, trying to be friendly.

"Yes, well, I have enemies on multiple sides," Smith continued in his squeaky, accented voice. "I try to always take time to thoroughly check out anyone who works for me. But I must admit you have arranged a lot of good deals for me in the past year."

Cam smiled. "Lucrative for us both."

"Glad to hear it." Another glance at Thompson.

Whatever silent communication was occurring between Smith and Thompson was causing alarms in Cameron's head. It was as if Smith kept asking Thompson for permission to talk, or checking to make sure what he said was okay. Which made absolutely no sense whatsoever.

Unless…

All of a sudden everything clicked in place for Cameron. Before he could help himself he straightened in his chair and looked over at Thompson. Really looked. And found the man studying him in much the same way.

Mr. Smith seemed oblivious to it all and kept talking. "We really appreciate the work you've done for us. And I thought it was time to bring you up here to meet me and a few more of my associates—"

"It's okay, Jacob, you can stop. I think Mr. Cameron has figured out our little ruse."

Cameron heard a slight indrawn breath from Sophia. Evidently she had noticed something, too.

"Sorry, Mr. Smith," the other, squeaky-voiced Mr. Smith said. "I was thrown off a little bit by the woman being here."

"Don't worry about it, Jacob," Thompson told the other man, who was getting up from the desk chair and giving his seat to Thompson. "The lovely Ms. Reardon could distract any man."

Thompson sat and turned to Cameron and Sophia. "You'll have to excuse all the subterfuge. I have found over the years that when meeting someone new, sometimes a stand-in is my best option. Jacob here has been with me for a long time. The idea came to me because both of our last names happen to be Smith. So when Jacob introduces himself as 'Mr. Smith,' that is actually the truth."

Cameron had to admit, it was a pretty great plan. And using someone like Jacob—lumpy, not very personable nor clever—probably gave Smith a distinct edge when dealing with others. Most people would do as Cameron had initially done: write off Smith as not much of a threat. Because Jacob Smith wasn't much of a threat.

But Thompson Smith definitely was. *This* was the man Cameron had been waiting to meet; Cameron could feel it in his bones. Thompson Smith was the one who had killed his partner; the man Cameron had sworn he would bring to justice.

"And then, when I'm here with certain unknown guests, I like to pretend I'm some sort of butler. It allows me to better observe those around me. You'd be amazed what people will say and do when they think they're just around hired help." Thompson Smith shook his head with a tsk. Jacob—the other Mr. Smith—went to stand closer to the window, obviously no longer part of the conversation.

"I must admit, you figured it out quicker than most," Smith told Cameron.

"Uh, yeah. Well, that guy—" Cameron gestured toward

Jacob "—is obviously related to Fin. But Fin never mentioned that his uncle was the head of DS-13. I've known Fin for a long time now and I don't think that's something he'd keep to himself for too long." Cameron pulled his cover identity around him like a blanket. It was time to be Cam Cameron now—kind of bright and organized, but not too much of either. The last thing Cameron wanted to do was put Smith on the defensive. This whole thing was already precariously balanced.

Smith seemed to buy it. "Yes, Fin has always loved to run his mouth." He then turned to study Sophia. "You, Ms. Reardon, have caused somewhat of a brouhaha around here."

Cameron forced himself not to tense up. It became more difficult as the seconds ticked by and Sophia didn't respond. Cameron shifted in his chair as casually as he could manage so he could glance over at Sophia. She was staring down silently at her hands folded in her lap.

Cameron didn't know how to help her. Was she overwhelmed and couldn't figure out how to respond? Afraid of messing up? Cameron was well aware that Sophia was not a trained agent. But if she was totally frozen and out of commission, things were about to spin out of control fast.

Cameron cleared his throat and gave a little laugh. "Sophia here is a little tired…."

Cameron didn't get out the rest of his sentence as Sophia looked up from her hands and at Mr. Smith. "Yeah, I tend to cause a little bit of a brouhaha no matter where I go."

Mr. Smith chuckled slightly and Cameron barely succeeded in keeping his jaw from dropping.

"I imagine you do, Ms. Reardon. We weren't expecting your presence here or in the warehouse yesterday," Smith told her.

"I gathered that from the multiple times your men threatened to kill me." Sophia looked Smith right in the eye as she said it.

Smith reached down to his desk and held up a file. "We did a little checking on you, of course. As I said, vetting everyone I come in contact with is standard procedure."

Sophia nodded. "Find anything interesting?"

Cameron had to give it to Sophia, she was handling herself like a pro. No nervous giveaways. Maybe it was possible they would make it out of this room alive.

"Nothing in particular. Except perhaps for the fact that you work for the FBI."

Damn.

Cameron flew out of his chair as if he had received an electric shock. "What? She's FBI? I swear I didn't know, Mr. Smith. She just said she knew something about this Ghost Shell thing and that you would want to hear it."

"It's all right, Cam. Ms. Reardon works for the FBI, but as a graphic artist, not an agent."

"Oh." Cameron sat back down slowly, feigning shock. "That's okay?"

"As soon as Fin reported that you had brought Sophia here back to the house in DC, I had her thoroughly checked out. Actually, having a record that so clearly linked her to the FBI helped ease my concerns a bit. Nobody trying to work undercover would be so easily linked to the FBI."

Smith turned and looked at Sophia. "And so you are still alive, my beautiful Sophia. And now there's no need to keep your FBI connection a secret."

Cameron didn't like how Smith was looking at her at all, but knew he couldn't do anything about it. Saying anything would just draw undue, and definitely unwanted, attention.

"Yeah, well, your henchmen didn't really seem like the type to take anyone associated with the Bureau to meet you," Sophia said.

Smith nodded. "Yes, and I must admit, if Fin had been able to get in touch with me yesterday, I would've denied him permission to bring you here. And what a shame that would've been. So, although I had to have some harsh words with Fin about security, I'm glad we had a little lapse today so I could meet you."

Sophia shifted uncomfortably in her chair.

"But, on to business." Smith leaned back in his chair. "Fin and Cam tell me you have particular knowledge about the Ghost Shell technology."

Here came the real test. Cameron's breath stuck in his throat.

"That's right." Sophia nodded. "And for the right price I'm willing to give that information to you."

Smith folded his hands on his desk. "Why don't you tell me exactly what you know, so I can determine what that information is worth."

Sophia mimicked Smith's relaxed pose, but with her hands in her lap. "I don't think so. I'm sure as soon as I do that my life won't be worth much. I'm not as stupid as some of the morons you surround yourself with around here." Sophia made a vague gesture toward Cameron.

Cameron sat up straighter in his chair. There wasn't much he could do to help her, but this was one thing: insulted lover. "Hey, I'm not a moron."

Smith chuckled and gave Cameron his attention. "Well, you certainly can pick them, Cam."

Cameron decided defensiveness was his best play. "I was just looking for a good time. Then I found out she knew some stuff about that Ghost Shell thing and told Fin she should tell you about it. That's it. I'm not, like, vouching for her or anything."

"Look, Cam was just the most attractive foot in the door

for me. One of your other hired thugs was my next option, but not as appealing—no offense."

Smith didn't move from his casual position. "Is that so? I understand there was quite a bit of carrying on in Cam's room at the house last night, including screaming."

Sophia shrugged delicately. "What can I say? I like it rough. Cam does, too."

"That worked out well for both of you, then." Smith laughed crassly.

Cameron chuckled, too, although he felt a little sick when he thought about the circumstances that had led to Sophia's screams back at the house. He glanced at her again. Her jaw had definitely tightened, but she gave nothing else away.

"Tell me, Sophia," Smith said after a few moments, "as delightful as you are, what is keeping me from just forcing the answer from you? I'm sure my men could find a way to be rougher than even you like."

Sophia sat up straighter in her chair, as did Cameron. The threat of torture wasn't to be taken lightly.

Out of the blue, Smith slammed his fist down on the desk, causing both Sophia and Cameron to startle. "You will tell me right now what you know." He never raised his voice, but his lower tone was all the more frightening.

Cameron prayed Sophia wouldn't panic. They were in too deep now.

"Ghost Shell has a fail-safe," Sophia said, barely above a whisper. "A code that has to be entered to make it work outside of its design parameters."

Smith nodded, but his eyes were icy. "Go on."

"You probably know Ghost Shell was designed by a government contractor. To keep it from being used against the US government, a fail-safe code was created. If someone tries to use Ghost Shell without the code, it won't work."

Cameron was impressed. That sounded realistic even to his ears, and he knew the truth. Too bad whoever had created Ghost Shell hadn't thought of something similar.

"There's only one chance to enter the code. You have to do it at a certain time, in a certain order and even in a certain tempo. Anything is off in the pattern and you've basically got a useless piece of junk on your hands."

Cameron almost missed Smith's glance over at the wall to his left. A small tell, but definitely a tell. Ghost Shell was probably in a safe there. And Smith was believing Sophia's story.

Smith glared at Sophia. "You're playing a very dangerous game here, Ms. Reardon."

"I'm not playing any games. I just want to get paid. Two million dollars. I know how much Ghost Shell is worth, and the amount I want from you is a fraction of that."

Smith's lips flattened and his nostrils flared the slightest bit. Cameron knew they were walking an even more precarious edge than he had thought.

Sophia glanced at her watch. "It's too late to enter the code today. The deadline has passed. That much I'll tell you in good faith."

Smith nodded and Sophia continued, "Tomorrow night I will enter the code for you. I'll get half the money before, and half afterward. Everyone can walk away happy from this, Mr. Smith."

Smith seemed to relax, and Cameron imagined it was because the amount Sophia was asking really was minute compared to Ghost Shell's black market value. But his eyes remained cold. "All right, Ms. Reardon, we have a deal. Tonight you and Cam will join me and my guests for the soiree, and tomorrow we shall deal with the business end of things."

Cameron nodded. "Sounds good."

"Just remember—" Smith leaned forward on his desk, menace clear on his face "—if you are lying to me, Sophia, about any part of this, you will beg for death before you finally die. That much I'll tell *you* in good faith."

Cameron watched as the color seeped from Sophia's face. She flinched when Smith repeated her words back at her.

Before their eyes, Smith's menace vanished and he was back to being the handsome host. He stood and Cameron and Sophia took their cue from him, and they all began walking toward the office door.

"Sophia, I assume the clothes I had brought in for you are acceptable?" Smith asked as if he hadn't threatened to torture and kill her just moments before.

Sophia nodded a little jerkily. "Yes, thank you." The words came out as a whisper.

"I hope you enjoy the gown I had picked out for you for this evening's festivities. It will suit your coloring and figure well, I believe," Smith said, reaching out to touch her on her elbow. Sophia seemed frozen.

Cameron was close enough to Sophia to see her pale and feel the fine tremor run through her body. He knew she wouldn't be able to hold it together much longer. He put himself between her and Smith.

"Yeah, thanks," Cam told Smith, struggling with all his might to grin. "She would've looked funny at the party running around in my shirt and pants." Cam ushered Sophia out the door. He turned back to Smith. "It was really great to finally meet you, Mr. Smith. And I hope you'll remember that I got Sophia here and helped save the day with Ghost Shell."

Smith nodded. "I won't forget your association with Sophia. It won't bode well for you, either, if she's lying."

"Oh, she's not, I'm sure," Cameron said, trying to put him at ease. "We'll see you tonight at the party."

Smith nodded and turned back into the office. Cameron took Sophia's arm and headed down the hall, grateful nobody was accompanying them. Sophia's breath was becoming more labored.

"Hang in there, baby," Cam whispered. "Just till we get back to the room."

They made it across the house to their room, with Cameron supporting most of Sophia's slight weight by the end. Cameron had barely closed the door before Sophia beelined to the bathroom and threw up everything she had eaten.

Chapter Eleven

Sophia felt relatively confident that she would never live through this day. Cameron kept praising her quietly, telling her what a remarkable job she had done with Smith, but Sophia just felt exhausted. They still couldn't talk freely because of the bug that Thompson—or Mr. Smith or whatever you wanted to call him—had placed in their room. That man gave her the freak-outs.

After she had completely lost the contents of her stomach, Cameron had helped Sophia from the bathroom, onto the bed. He was sitting beside her, stroking her hair back from her face, as he had been for the past twenty minutes.

"I wouldn't worry too much about what Mr. Smith said," Cameron told her in a voice loud enough for the surveillance to clearly hear him. "You'll just give him the information tomorrow, he'll pay you and it will be all over."

"Yeah…" The word came out all croaky so Sophia started again. "Yeah, I just don't like people threatening to kill me."

A knock on the door brought them both to attention. Sophia stayed where she was as Cameron went to open the door. It was Fin carrying two separate hanging bags of clothes. He was also sporting a nasty bruise on his jaw.

"These are from Mr. Smith," Fin said gruffly, thrusting the bags into Cameron's arms.

"Which one? Your uncle or the real Mr. Smith?" Cameron scoffed. "What happened to your face, Fin?"

"Your girlfriend is what happened to my face. Mr. Smith didn't like it that I allowed Sophia to arrive with us without contacting him first, even though she has something he wants," Fin spat. A vein pulsed in his neck as he turned to glare at Sophia on the bed. "You should've told me you were FBI."

Sophia recoiled from the venom in Fin's eyes. "I'm not really FBI. I just happen to work at the FBI building. Plus, I'm sure you would've just killed me if I had mentioned it."

Fin didn't respond to that, just turned and marched out the door. Cameron unzipped and held up the contents of the bags. One contained dress pants and a light gray shirt for Cameron. The other contained a black gown that looked quite lovely and demure in the front. But then Sophia turned it around on the hanger and saw that it was backless almost down to the waist.

Sophia cringed. It was beautiful, but definitely not something she would've ever picked out or worn. "Looks like we have our costumes for tonight."

Cameron nodded. "You okay?"

"I don't like having to wear what he picks out for me. But I guess it's better than a shirt and jeans." Sophia turned and went into the bathroom to build her resolve. If this dress was her only option then she'd make the best of it.

A couple hours later they were on their way to the main part of the house. Sophia was glad to be out of the room—having to monitor every word that came out of their mouths was stressful. She was constantly worried she was going to let something slip.

The dress was on, fitting her perfectly. Her hair was up in a sophisticated twist. She'd made full use of the makeup that had arrived with the dress. Sophia knew she looked good.

But she hated every bit of it.

Even seeing Cameron's expression when she had walked out of the bathroom—and Sophia had to admit that watching his jaw almost drop to the ground had been pretty thrilling—she still wished she wasn't wearing this dress.

Or that she was wearing it under very different circumstances.

She and Cameron made their way to the main section of the house, where people were already milling around and talking. The sun had set, taking with it the gorgeous views outside, but the party room itself was beautiful enough.

They joined the crowd, talking and mingling with different people. Sophia received multiple compliments on the dress, which she barely acknowledged. And she absolutely hated the way Smith had nodded with approval when he had seen her in it. She didn't think Cameron noticed. He was busy thinking like an agent.

"I wish I had facial-recognition software here, or at least a camera," Cameron grumbled as they moved through more people. "I know there are people here that Omega should be aware are associates of Smith's. But I'm pretty useless."

"I might be able to help a little bit," Sophia told him. "Obviously I can't remember everyone, but if you see a few people who you want to remember, I can study them and draw them later."

"Really?" Cameron smiled down at her. "That would be unbelievably helpful."

Finally something Sophia could do that would be helpful. Good. She was tired of feeling like an albatross.

She and Cameron wandered around chatting, watching Smith and who he interacted with. As Cameron would signal to her about a certain person to remember, Sophia would do her best to memorize features. Sophia felt so much more comfortable doing that than trying to convince Smith she knew some secret information about some computer virus or whatever. Studying people, remembering features, drawing them, even days or weeks later—*that* she could do.

But Sophia definitely didn't like the way Smith would look at her whenever he could meet her eyes. As if he owned her.

The veiled malevolence in Smith's eyes wouldn't be easy to capture in a drawing. Sophia hoped she never had to try. She didn't even want to think about tomorrow when she wasn't able to put in any sort of password.

What had Smith said? That she would beg for death before she finally died? Amazing how that would sound so melodramatic under any other circumstances, but sounded so credible coming from Smith. Glancing at him again across the room Sophia could easily imagine he knew many ways to make someone beg for death.

Sophia could feel nausea pooling again in her stomach.

"You doing okay?" Cameron whispered.

"Smith." She gestured toward the older man with a tilt of her head. "He makes me nervous."

"If he keeps looking at you like that, things might get ugly around here really quick," Cameron said.

Sophia shivered. "I know. Can we just get out of here? Do we have to stay for the entire evening?"

"No. We don't have to stay. As a matter of fact, I think I have an even better plan than staying here." Cameron smiled at her in a way that made Sophia's insides start to melt.

Sophia swallowed hard. The only options were basically staying here or going back to the bedroom. Was that what Cameron wanted?

Sophia knew that was what she wanted. If there was one thing she had learned from this whole…*adventure*, it was that you never knew how many days you had left. Especially when someone waited in the wings looking for an excuse to kill you.

She hadn't made love with Cameron five years ago because she thought she'd had all the time in the world. That ended up not being true. She wouldn't make the same mistake now, especially when tomorrow hung so very precariously in the balance.

Sophia smiled up at Cameron. "Okay, I'm ready to go whenever you are."

He reached down and squeezed her hand. "All right, we should stay here a little bit longer, then we can start to make our way out as inconspicuously as possible."

His smile took her breath away. Sophia never thought she could feel this way in a situation like this. Just for tonight she wasn't going to worry about tomorrow. Because she didn't even know if she'd have a tomorrow.

Cameron subtly started angling them toward one of the doors. They spoke briefly with a few people as they made their way out and Cameron stopped to tell Fin they were leaving. She noticed Cameron awkwardly bump into Fin when a waiter came by. Cameron apologized, but Fin stormed off to the other end of the room. Obviously Fin was still mad at them for getting him in trouble with Mr. Smith. Sophia was glad when they didn't go anywhere near Mr. Smith to say their goodbyes; he was busy talking to other people anyway.

Once they made it out of the main room, Sophia finally felt as if she could breathe without panic pushing at her chest. She just wanted to get back to the room.

Cameron wrapped an arm around her and hugged her to his side. "Thank you for doing this."

Okay, odd. "Um, you're welcome."

"We're not going to have much time, so we'll need to hurry."

Now Sophia was really confused. "Why? Are you ex-pecting them to come barging into our bedroom?"

"No," Cameron told her as he walked quickly with her down the hallway. "I mean breaking into Smith's office while everyone's at the party to see if we can find Ghost Shell."

SOPHIA HAD SOME sort of strange look on her face and Cam-eron couldn't blame her. Not with the way Smith had been looking at her all evening. Cameron didn't blame Soph for wanting to get out of there.

Cameron had that itchy feeling on the back of his neck all evening—the one that told him things were not going the way he'd planned. He didn't get the feeling very often, but over the years, first as a US Army Ranger then as an undercover agent, he had learned to pay attention to it.

Things were about to take a turn for the worse.

During this party, while everybody was occupied, was the best time to try to get into Smith's office and get Ghost Shell. Once they had that, Cameron could get Sophia out, on foot if he had to.

The more time he spent with her, the more he was com-ing to realize how much she meant to him. He wanted to get this case finished as soon as possible. And he could admit Sophia was his primary reason for that.

He wanted to be with her outside of this lunatic situa-tion. Cameron glanced at Sophia as they walked down the hall. The strange look was gone. Now she seemed focused and determined to get the job done. Her grit was down-right sexy.

But hell, everything about her was sexy. Especially in that almost-backless dress she was wearing. Cameron hated that Smith had picked it out, but had to admit Smith's choice was flawless.

They quietly made their way back to the locked door of Smith's office. Cameron pulled out a swipe card for the lock and held it up. He had taken it from Fin a few minutes ago when he had bumped into him. "Not a good day for Fin. We're probably going to get him fired."

Sophia snickered. "My heart breaks for him."

Cameron closed the door behind them but left it cracked just a little so they could get out quickly if they needed to.

"Okay, so what exactly are we looking for?" Sophia asked him as she made her way over to the desk. Cameron was right behind her.

"Ghost Shell is an external hard drive. The encryption device contains too much data to fit on anything too small, so it's about the size of a hardback book."

Sophia pulled out the desk chair, sat down and began searching through drawers on one side of the desk. Cameron began looking around a wall of bookshelves.

"It's not going to be in a drawer just out in the open," Cameron said softly. "I saw Smith looking over at this wall earlier when we were talking about Ghost Shell. There must be a safe."

Cameron continued to look around the wall, but couldn't find anything. Every minute they were in this office put them in more danger. He quickly joined Sophia at the desk and started to feel around. He ran his hands along the sides of it then under the writing surface. Sure enough, a button lay hidden in the corner. No one would ever know it was there unless they were looking for it.

"I've got it." Cameron pressed the button and watched as one panel of books began to move.

They both saw it at the same time. A lamp that had been placed in front of the panel to make it less conspicuous.

"Cam, the lamp!"

Sophia and Cameron both dived for it, but were too late. The lamp fell to the floor with a loud crash.

Damn.

The crash seemed deafening in the otherwise silent room. All color drained from Sophia's face.

"What do we do?" She looked around frantically.

Was it possible that nobody had heard the lamp fall? In the party nobody would have heard it, but was anyone nearby? Cameron held his breath, then cursed when he heard a door open down the hall. Someone was coming, blocking their only route of escape.

It was too late to get them anywhere safe. Cameron looked at Sophia, who was watching him with a fully panicked look in her eyes.

Cameron burst into a flurry of activity. He pushed the button to close the panel in front of the safe, then quickly picked up the lamp that had fallen to the hardwood floor— thankfully, it hadn't broken—and put it back on the shelf in front of the closed panel.

He grabbed a crystal vase that rested on the desk and put it on the floor. Sophia just watched him, not understanding at all what he was trying to do.

She looked even more shocked when he began unbuttoning his dress shirt, pulling it from where it was tucked into his pants. Then he lifted her by the waist and set her on the desk. Before Sophia could ask what he was doing, Cameron climbed on top of the desk and began kissing her.

Cameron peeled her dress as far down one shoulder as it would go, baring a great deal of skin. He threaded his fingers in her hair and pushed her back fully on the desk. He pulled up one of her legs and hooked it around his waist and slid his hand over her breast, grabbing it roughly.

He heard Sophia whimper against his mouth in protest of the hard kiss and felt her pull her torso away from him.

Cameron opened his eyes to find her wide green eyes staring at him.

She was frightened.

Cameron stopped immediately. He couldn't stand that look in her eyes. True, Cameron was trying to put on a show for whoever was about to come through that door, but this was Sophia. He didn't want her frightened of being close to him.

He brought his hand back up to stroke her cheek. He leaned his weight on his elbows and gazed gently down at her.

"Sorry, baby," he whispered, and stroked her cheek once more. "Let's try this again, slower. Kiss me."

This time Cameron brought his lips gently down to hers. He teased her bottom lip with his nipping little kisses, then gave the same attention to the upper one. He heard Sophia sigh and watched as her eyes closed.

Cameron deepened the kiss as Sophia responded. Her arms came up and wrapped around his neck. A knot of need twisted in him as he drew her closer.

Cameron tried to remind himself that this was all an act, that any moment now someone from DS-13 would walk through the door and have to believe that the only thing going on in here was hot sex. But as he kissed Sophia again he realized that there was no acting about it.

This time when Cameron's hand moved onto her beautiful body again it was because he couldn't stop himself, not because he wanted to put on any sort of show. Cameron shifted so he could get closer to Sophia. She moaned and held on to him, her fingers threading through his hair.

Just a few moments later the door to the office flew open and the lights flipped on.

It was Rick. Damn it. And he had his weapon in his hand.

"What the hell are you doing in here?"

Cameron subtly shifted so he was blocking more of Sophia from Rick's view.

"What the hell does it look like we're doing, Rick? Get out."

But Rick wasn't backing down. "You're not supposed to be in here."

Cameron decided to try a different route. "Dude, we're just having a little fun in the boss's room. You know, a little danger." He gave Rick a knowing grin. *"Capiche?"*

Rick's dark eyes narrowed. Cameron didn't know what the younger man was going to do. If Rick decided to get Mr. Smith, things would become much more complicated.

"Let me off this desk." Sophia pushed out from under him. "I told you we should just go back to the room, jackass."

Sophia wiggled completely out from under him and straightened her dress over her body, but not before Rick caught a glimpse of some tantalizing flesh, Cameron was sure. She looked over at Rick without flinching. "What's the matter with you, never seen a woman before?" she snapped at him with a jutting chin. She turned to Cam. "Can we please go back to the room now? I don't like having an audience. At least, not him."

Cameron watched as Sophia began to walk toward the door. Whatever suspicions Rick had were obviously lost as he looked at Sophia with cruel lust in his eyes.

Rick grabbed her arm as she walked by. "Maybe you and I will get our turn soon." Cameron could see Sophia wince, but he didn't intervene.

Fighting a man with a gun in his hand would not work out well for any of them. Plus, it would be completely out of character for Cam Cameron. Instead, Cameron leaned down and put the vase he'd set on the floor earlier back on the desk.

"Yeah, I don't think so." Sophia all but spat the words.

Rick grabbed her other arm and pulled her up against him fully. "We'll see about that."

Cameron walked over casually. "All right, Romeo, that's enough. We'll see you in the morning."

Rick smirked, but he stepped back so they could get through the doorway.

Cameron wasn't sure what Rick's weird smile was all about, but he wasn't sticking around to find out. They had dodged a bullet, literally and figuratively. Cameron grabbed Sophia's arm and they made their escape.

Chapter Twelve

As they reached their room, Cameron signaled for Sophia to wait right inside the door. The bug was still there. It was time to get rid of that thing.

He just hoped that Rick would keep his mouth shut about seeing them. Cameron supposed it was possible. The way Sophia had shunned Rick, he probably wouldn't want to announce that to anyone very soon.

Frustration gnawed in Cameron's gut. They had been so close to finding Ghost Shell. If they had just had a few more minutes—and if that stupid lamp hadn't fallen—he could've cracked the safe. Then he could've gotten Sophia, and the device, out of here.

Which was what was best, Cameron knew. But after what happened on the desk, Cameron was torn between wanting her to go and wanting her to stay.

Basically just plain wanting her.

He wanted her still. It was physical, definitely, the desire he had for her. But after the way she'd totally kept it together over the past forty-eight hours, it was more than that. Cameron found himself realizing that Sophia had courage and backbone, things he never knew she had. He suspected she never knew she possessed those qualities, either.

And her strengths were so very attractive to him. Everything about her was becoming more and more attractive to him.

And the way she had kissed him back on the desk… There was definitely an attraction and it was definitely affecting both of them. And Cameron planned to do something about it.

But first they needed to talk. That definitely could not happen with the bug still in the room. Cameron walked over to the tray. Sophia stood just inside the door, seeming unsure as to what she should do.

Cameron took the tray and set it on the floor out in the hallway, closing the door again behind him. He signaled for Sophia to remain quiet as he got out his Omega equipment and made sure no other bugs had been placed in the room while they were gone.

None. Finally, a break.

"Now we can talk." Cameron didn't speak at full volume, but at least they didn't have to speak in low tones.

"Won't they wonder about the tray?"

"I'll tell them there was a funny smell and it was bugging me."

Sophia smiled crookedly. "Okay."

"Are you all right?" Cameron walked over to her, stopping just short of touching her.

"Do you mean in general or after what just happened?"

"Both, I guess. But specifically I was referring to what happened a few minutes ago."

Sophia shook her head. "You mean Rick? I guess I shouldn't have egged him on. But I couldn't help it. That guy gives me the creeps."

"Yeah, no kidding. Rick definitely has a cruel side." Cameron saw Sophia shudder. "But I was actually talking about what happened between you and me. On the desk."

Sophia took a step back from Cameron, then turned

and walked over to the bed, sitting down on the edge. She didn't speak for a long moment. "Don't worry about it, Cam. I understand."

"Well, explain it to me, because I don't understand." Cameron didn't like the way she was looking down, as if she was too embarrassed to make eye contact with him.

"At the desk, you were undercover. You thought fast. It was a good plan, and it worked. It seemed to fool Rick."

"Sophia—"

"I get it, Cam, I really do. It was like earlier when I came out of the bathroom and you kissed me. Again, smart, quick thinking on your part. You probably saved our lives."

She looked up at him then, and shrugged her shoulders wearily. Cameron most distinctly did not like what he saw in her eyes: wariness, embarrassment, resignation. He walked closer to her, but she held out an arm to stop him.

"There's no need to keep up the pretense now, Cam. There's no bug in the room or creep coming down the hall about to catch us where we're not supposed to be."

Sophia stood up. "I'm going to take another bath, okay?"

Cameron had heard enough. He strode purposely over to Sophia and threaded both his hands into her hair. He tilted her head back so he could look directly into her eyes. A shocked sound came out of her throat at his sudden movement.

"Let's get something straight here, Soph. Yes, I am undercover and yes, this situation is beyond complicated."

"Listen, Cam…" Sophia tried to step back, but Cameron wouldn't let her.

"No, you listen. I have to be *on*, all the time here. My life, your life, the success of the mission, getting justice for my partner, all depend on me staying focused."

Sophia dropped her gaze. "I *know*, Cam. I understand that."

Cameron bent his knees so he could catch her eyes again. When she finally looked at him, he continued, "Well, know and understand this—you blow my focus all to hell. I want you in a way I have never wanted any other woman."

That got her attention. "Wh-what?"

"You really think I'm just acting when I kiss you, acting during what happened on the desk?"

"You're not?" Her shocked tone told him all he needed to know.

"Baby, if Rick hadn't come into that office, we'd still be on that desk. Hell, I should probably thank Rick so that I won't forever have to try to forget that our first time was on the desk of the man who killed my partner."

"It's just so hard for me to tell, Cam. To know what's real and what's not with you."

Cameron brought his lips down to hers and kissed her gently. "Know this is real," he whispered against her lips.

He felt the moment Sophia gave in to the kiss. Her arms came up and entwined around his neck. Cameron bent his knees again so he could wrap his arms around her waist, then lifted her so she was face-to-face with him.

"You always were a tiny little thing," he told her, still kissing her.

Her arms wrapped more firmly around his neck. "I'll have you know, I'm the absolute perfect size."

"Oh, I don't doubt that at all, Ms. Reardon." Cameron began backing up until her legs rested against the side of the bed, then lowered her feet back to the ground. He trailed kisses down the side of her neck and delighted as it caused her to break out in goose bumps. He reached down and slid both sleeves of her dress off her shoulders, and because of its open back, it slid to the floor and pooled at her feet.

"Perfect size, indeed," he murmured as he removed his own shirt.

"Cameron..." He loved the sound of her voice as she said his name.

Cameron stood and picked her up again, lowering her onto the bed slowly and with a great deal more finesse than he had before. His mouth found hers again. Her hands clenched into his shoulders.

Cameron wanted to take things slow, to make sure not to frighten her as he had on the desk. Cameron moved on top of her, propping his weight up on his elbows, holding back. But evidently Sophia had other plans.

She pulled his weight down to her, making quick work of removing his clothes and the rest of hers. Passion was building to a fevered pitch. This was definitely real; no acting involved whatsoever.

That was Cameron's last coherent thought before he lost himself in the fervor and heat that consumed both he and Sophia.

THE NEXT MORNING Sophia made good use of the giant bathroom again, this time to take a shower. Cameron had joined her in there—good thing there had been more than room enough for two—although him joining her had greatly prolonged the length of the shower.

They were both toweling off now, in the steam-filled bathroom. "I so don't want to ask this, but did Smith provide any more clothes? Anything casual?" Sophia didn't want to put on the ball gown again or yesterday's dress pants.

"I'll check." A few moments later Cameron, having gotten dressed in jeans and a soft black sweater, brought in a new package and set it on the counter. Sophia opened it, relieved to see a pair of jeans and a navy blue T-shirt. Underclothes, socks and a pair of casual shoes completed Smith's wardrobe for Sophia today.

Sophia still hated having to wear what that psycho chose for her.

Speaking of psycho… "So what's our plan when I meet with him tonight for the code? I don't think I'm going to be able to bluff my way out again." A shudder went through her as she put on the jeans.

"I'm going to contact Omega and insist on an extraction for you this evening. Your life is definitely in jeopardy, so they won't refuse again."

"Just for me? You're not coming, too?"

"We'll see. If my cover's blown, then yes, I'll be extracted, too. No point staying here just to be tortured and killed."

Sophia rolled her eyes. "Some people have no sense of adventure."

Cameron gave a soft bark of laughter and walked over to kiss her. "We have a few hours. A lot can happen in that time. But either way, I'm getting you out before this goes any further. You'll never have to see Smith again."

Sophia felt as if a huge weight was lifted. Not having to see Smith again was just fine. She tried to pull the T-shirt on over her head and winced from the pain in her arm.

Cameron helped her bring her arm back down, staring at the jagged cut on her shoulder and upper arm from the nail. "That's starting to look pretty infected. Does it hurt?"

Although she hadn't really noticed it in the midst of last night's activities or in the shower this morning, Sophia could definitely feel an ache now. She looked over at the wound. The skin around where she had scraped against the rusty nail was puffy and a fiery red.

"It's a little sore, but not unmanageable."

"When was your last tetanus shot?"

Sophia had no idea. It wasn't something she thought about regularly. "I don't know. High school, maybe?"

Cameron grimaced. "That's not great, but it's still within the ten-year mark. Let's get that bandaged." He helped her up to sit on the marble bathroom counter.

Cameron applied an antibacterial ointment and began wrapping her arm in gauze, both items from his duffel bag.

"You're like a Boy Scout with that duffel bag of yours."

Cameron smiled and winked at her. "I try to keep as much in there as I can without carrying anything that would arouse suspicion if someone goes through it."

"Do they go through your bags a lot?"

"I don't know, but I never assume that they don't. I stay more alive that way. So yeah, I have a lot of junk in there. It helps camouflage the important stuff."

"Like that cell phone thing you used to communicate with Omega?"

"It wasn't actually a cell phone, but yes. Like that." He finished wrapping her shoulder. "Okay, you're all patched up."

He helped Sophia ease the shirt over her head. Sophia tried not to provide any indication at all that her arm was hurting her. Then she forgot all about any pain as Cameron grabbed her by the hips and scooted her to the edge of the counter and kissed her.

"Remind me again why we didn't do this five years ago?" he whispered against her lips.

Sophia smiled. "If we had known it would be this good, I don't think we'd have been able to wait."

Sophia thought about Cameron when she had known him before. She had been finishing college then, with her degree in graphic design. He had just been coming out of the US Army Rangers and had told her he wasn't sure what he was going to do with his life.

Sophia pulled back from him. "You lied to me before.

You told me you didn't know what profession you'd end up in."

Cameron made a *hmm* noise in his throat. "I didn't really lie to you."

Sophia lifted a single eyebrow.

Cameron had the good grace to at least look sheepish. "Yeah, Omega approached me while I was still in the army, so I knew I was going to work for them. But I wasn't sure exactly how I would fit in with the organization and what I would be doing. So I wasn't technically lying…"

"You know, for a while after you left, since you didn't say a real goodbye or anything, I thought it was because I hadn't had sex with you," Sophia whispered.

"What?" Cameron's head jerked back.

Sophia shrugged. "Well, for the first couple months with all our breakfasts together, I knew you didn't expect anything. But when things started building between us and we started going out on dates and stuff…"

"Let me get this straight." Cameron's jaw clenched and his eyes tightened. He removed his hands from Sophia's waist and placed them on the counter on either side of her legs. "You thought I left because you didn't put out?"

Sophia tried not to let Cameron's looming chest intimidate her. She slid back on the counter a bit. "It was a possible theory, yes. After all, I had no idea why you had left, did I?" Sophia poked him in the big, looming chest.

"*That* had nothing to do with it."

"Yeah, well, I didn't know that. All I knew was everything seemed to be going fine between us and then all of a sudden you were gone. No goodbye from you, just a cryptic message on my phone when you knew I wouldn't be home."

Cameron's shoulders hunched. "Yeah, I guess you're right." There was a long pause. "I couldn't tell you about

Omega Sector, Soph. And they told me I had to break ties as cleanly as possible."

"You mean no one at Omega has any outside relationships? No marriages or anything like that? It seems a bit extreme."

"No, they do. A bunch of people are married and have families in Omega. It's just..." Cameron turned from facing her to leaning against the counter next to her.

"What?" Sophia asked when Cameron didn't keep talking.

"All casual ties had to be severed."

It took a second for the pain to set in, but when it did it stole Sophia's breath. What could she say to that? She had thought he was the one. He had thought of her as a casual tie.

"Oh," she finally managed to whisper.

"Soph, I'm sorry. I never thought of you—of what we had—as casual."

"But you told Omega Sector it was." It wasn't a question.

"They asked about the nature of our relationship. How long we'd been together and stuff like that. They needed to know how often I spent the night at your house. If I was going to work for Omega, and I was in a solid, committed relationship with you, then you'd have to be closely scrutinized, also."

Sophia waited but didn't say anything.

"On paper it looked like we had breakfast together all the time and had been on a few dates," he said softly.

"Casual," Sophia whispered.

"Soph, that time we spent together. All those mornings at the diner. The dates, the kisses. They were important to me, too."

"But not important enough to make you stay. Or to tell Omega that I wasn't a casual relationship."

Cameron was standing right next to her, but the gap between them was almost insurmountable. Sophia slid a little farther away from him on the counter. She was afraid if he touched her right now she might shatter into a million pieces.

Cameron pinched the bridge of his nose, his eyes closed. "If I could go back in time to five years ago, there are so many things I would do differently."

Chapter Thirteen

Cameron would give every paycheck he'd ever get for the rest of his life if he never had to see that look on Sophia's face ever again. He had known he'd screwed up when he walked away from her five years ago. But he had never dreamed it had hurt her as much as it had hurt him.

Cameron didn't know exactly what he had thought. Maybe that she would move on quickly because they hadn't been too physical. Maybe that she was young and that a clean break would be easy to recover from.

"I had to choose. At the time I thought I was making the right choice." Cameron knew he had to make her understand, but the right words seemed to fail him.

Sophia turned her head away and it almost broke his heart. "I understand," she whispered.

He grabbed her chin firmly and forced her to look at him. "I'm pretty sure you don't understand at all. There's not a day that goes by that I don't regret that decision." He sighed, releasing her chin and turning away. "But it's complicated. I know I've done a lot of good work with Omega— maybe even saved a lot of lives. But…"

Cameron wasn't even sure what the rest of that sentence was. Silence hung between them.

"But you wonder, deep inside, if it was worth the price you paid personally," Sophia finally said.

Yes, that summed it up perfectly. Sophia had always understood him.

"Every. Damn. Day." Cameron turned around to face her again. He reached up and trailed the back of his fingers down her cheek. "And always because of…"

They both jumped a bit at the pounding on the door.

Cameron reached over and kissed her briefly and went to answer their bedroom door. It was Fin.

"Mr. Smith wants to see you in his office to talk about business stuff. She—" he gestured at Sophia "—doesn't need to go."

"Right now? It's eight o'clock in the morning."

"Yes, now. Mr. Smith is an early riser."

There was nothing particularly bad about what Fin was saying, but Cameron still felt tension pooling in his stomach. "But Smith doesn't want to see Sophia?"

"No, just you. For stuff having nothing to do with her. She can stay here and somebody will bring a breakfast tray." Fin gave nothing away, probably because he knew nothing.

Cameron wasn't sure which way to push. He didn't want to be away from Sophia and leave her here by herself, but on the other hand keeping her as far from Smith as possible was probably the best plan.

"Okay," Cameron finally said. "I'll go to Mr. Smith's office in just a few minutes." Maybe it was time to get Sophia out of here right now.

"I'm supposed to wait for you right here and take you," Fin told him.

So much for getting Sophia out right now.

Did Smith know they had been in his office last night? Had Rick told them? Surely they would've already been summoned, *both* of them, if that was the case. Maybe this really was just a routine meeting to discuss details. Cameron nodded. "Give me just a second."

Cameron closed the door and Sophia came out of the bathroom. "Everything okay?"

"Yeah, I think. Fin just came to tell me Smith wants to meet with me."

Cameron could almost see the tension that flooded Sophia's body. "Why? Is there a problem? Do you think Rick told him about us in the office?"

"No. We'd have already been dragged in there if he had."

Sophia still looked worried. "Then what?"

"Just a meeting. After all, I am his employee. Business details, Fin said." Cameron walked over to his bag and got out the SIG he had hidden there. He tucked it into the back of his jeans. He hoped he wouldn't need it, but this close to getting Sophia out, he wasn't taking any chances.

"Do I come, too?"

"No. You're supposed to stay here. They're going to bring up a tray with some breakfast. Eat as much as you can."

"Okay." Sophia looked as hesitant about this plan as Cameron felt. He walked over to her and pulled her into his arms.

"Just hang in there a few more hours," he whispered into her ear. "Let me go act normal with Smith and I'll be back in a bit. Then we'll get you out of here."

Sophia reached up her hands to frame his face. "Be careful." She stood up on her tiptoes to kiss him.

Cameron stepped back after a few moments even though he wanted nothing more than to stay there in her embrace. "I will. Stay here in the room. Get the tray when it's delivered, but otherwise keep the door locked."

Sophia nodded and Cameron turned and walked out the door.

Fin was still waiting, as promised. They silently walked together to Smith's office.

Unlike yesterday, Cameron could tell Smith's office door was already open from down the hall. As they got closer, Cam could hear Smith talking—and laughing—with another man. Cameron walked into the office, Fin following right behind, but staying by the door. He obviously was still not in Smith's good graces.

"Cam, come in," Smith said good-naturedly.

Thompson Smith, when playing the role of DS-13 leader, looked polished and friendly, not at all like the butler Cameron had mistook him for yesterday. Having seen him play both roles, Cameron could understand how he had eluded law enforcement for years. But no matter which role he played, Smith's eyes were still cold and hard.

The eyes of a killer.

"Good morning, Mr. Smith. Fin said you wanted to meet with me about some business."

"Yes, yes." Smith nodded. "A few very important details. First, this is my associate Mr. McNeil. He came up this morning to discuss some business, also. Fred, this is Cam Cameron, about whom we were talking earlier."

Talking about him could be good or bad, Cam knew. He also noticed no details were provided by either men as to what type of "associate" McNeil was. But McNeil stuck out his hand for shaking, so Cameron assumed it was good. "Nice to meet you."

Cam shook the hand and responded, "You, too, man." McNeil faded over to the side of the room and propped himself up against the wall, obviously to get out of the way of whatever business Mr. Smith had with Cameron.

"I trust you had a good time at the party last night?" Smith asked.

Cameron tensed for just a moment then forced himself to

relax. Had he been wrong and Smith did know about them breaking into the office? If so, he'd have to think of a way to play this off quick. His best bet was probably to pretend to be the bad boy—wanting to have sex in the boss's office.

Disrespectful, sure. But better than announcing he was a federal agent.

"Yeah. Lots of fun. Plenty of trouble to get into," Cameron told him, providing what he hoped was a charming grin. Charming was hard to pull off when all you wanted to do was arrest the bastard sitting across from you and see that he rot in jail for the next 150 years or so.

"Yes, there's always lots of trouble with my parties." Smith chuckled. "And I trust our lovely Sophia had a good time, also? She looked beautiful last night."

Smith wasn't giving away much. Cam grinned again. "She didn't seem to have any complaints."

"Glad to hear that. Tell me a little more about Sophia. You seem quite taken with her. You met her for the first time a few days ago at the warehouse?"

These questions were not going in the direction Cameron had wanted. He couldn't quite determine their purpose. Did Smith know something? Was he setting up Cam? Or did he just like the sordid little details of other people's lives?

He wouldn't put any of it past Smith.

Cam decided to play it on the assumption that Smith didn't really know anything. It was his only real option anyway. To make up some sort of history between he and Sophia now would just be suspicious. "Yeah, at the warehouse, where Marco found her."

"And you think she was there to try to sell us the information she had about Ghost Shell."

"Yeah, that's what she told me. Honestly, really, I just thought she was hot. I wasn't thinking much past that." Better to come across as careless, rather than a traitor.

"But when Fin and Rick were about to eliminate her, you stopped them."

Cam looked at Smith then over at McNeil, who still was leaning against the wall. "Yeah, it seemed like a waste." Cam shrugged. "She knew stuff that was helpful about Ghost Shell so I thought we should bring her to you and let you decide."

"I see." Smith sat back in his chair.

"I mean, I know she wants you to pay her money, Mr. Smith. But at least Ghost Shell will still work with her help. And it sounded like you would make much more from selling it than what she was asking." Cameron injected a bit of nervousness into his tone, which wasn't difficult.

"Yes, that's true," Smith responded, leaning back in his chair. "The problem is that I have Mr. McNeil here, who tells me that the information Sophia provided was not correct."

Cameron looked over at Fred McNeil. "Oh, okay. Are you a computer specialist guy or something?" Cam added just a little bit of mockery. Perhaps he could discredit this guy. But it was a long shot.

Fred snorted. "No. I am definitely not any type of computer geek."

"Then how do you know that Sophia isn't telling the truth?"

Mr. Smith answered for Fred. "Because Mr. McNeil is on my payroll and has been for years. He works for the FBI."

This was not what Cameron wanted to hear on multiple levels. First, because a mole selling secrets to DS-13 was never good, but more important, because this meant Sophia was really in trouble. Tonight was going to be too late to get her out. She'd be dead long before then.

Cameron shot from his chair. "Whoa. FBI? I don't want

to have anything to do with an FBI agent." He had to stall. Figure out what to do.

His sudden movement had put McNeil on the defensive. His hand was already at his weapon.

"Calm down, Cam," Smith told him. "Obviously, Fred is not here to arrest anyone. He wouldn't be much use to me if he was, would he?"

Cam pretended to process that. He sat back down slowly. "No, I guess not." He glared over at Fred. "Sorry. Not a big fan of law enforcement."

Fred just rolled his eyes and Cam could tell that he'd just written Cameron off as being just another dumb thug. Good.

But Smith didn't seem quite as quick to lump Cam in that category. "Fred informs me that what Sophia said about some secret fail-safe code is not accurate."

"Maybe she knows something he doesn't."

Fred pushed himself away from the wall and came to stand closer to Smith's desk. "Look, Sophia Reardon is a *graphic artist* for the FBI. She's not an agent. She's not in the cyberterrorism division. She made up all that crap about a special code."

"How do you know?" Cameron asked.

"Because I was the person who acquired Ghost Shell for DS-13," Fred sneered. "Some goody-goody computer scientist at a technology company contacted us a few months ago in fear that something like Ghost Shell was being developed. Guess who happened to be assigned that call?"

"You?" That would explain a lot. How Ghost Shell got into DS-13's hands so quickly. And why the FBI was so clueless. The FBI may not even officially know that Ghost Shell existed. Omega Sector knew of its existence, but Omega had resources and connections the Bureau didn't have.

Agent McNeil rolled his eyes. "Yes, obviously. Me. So

when I say your lady friend is lying, I know what I'm talking about. I know things that are going on in the FBI, the CIA and even some agencies you've never even heard of."

Things had just gone from bad to hell-in-a-handbasket. Obviously discrediting Agent McNeil wasn't going to work. And his bragging about unknown agencies—was McNeil referring to Omega? A mole in Omega would be ugly. Life-threatening, not only to Cameron, but also multiple other agents. Agents that included his family and friends.

Mr. Smith stood up. "Fin, get Rick and have him fetch Ms. Reardon and bring her here." Smith smiled over at Agent McNeil. "Rick has a nice cruel streak I find useful in these types of situations."

Cameron didn't turn around as he heard the door click behind him. He had to do something, fast. But pulling his SIG out now wouldn't do anything but get him killed.

"You were the one we couldn't figure out, Cam." Smith turned his attention back to Cameron. "Whether you were working with Ms. Reardon to cheat me of money."

Cam held his hands out in front of him. "Whoa. I just met this chick a couple of days ago! I thought I was helping you, Mr. Smith, honest. I had no idea she was trying to scam you."

Smith walked over to one of his large bookshelves. "I actually believe you, Cam. Not because of what you're saying right now, but because given the timeline of the development and our acquisition of Ghost Shell and Fin's ability to account for your location during that time, I believe you when you say you just met Ms. Reardon. Although I must admit, I hope you're not too fond of her, given what's about to happen."

Cameron watched as Smith reached over, pulled down a book from the bookshelf and opened it. Inside was a cleverly hidden keypad and biometrics scanner, into which

Smith punched a code and provided his thumbprint. The entire bookshelf spun and opened.

This was much more than the safe he and Sophia had found last night. And with the security measures Smith had, there was no way they would've been able to break in. Obviously he and Sophia hadn't been as close to discovering Ghost Shell as Cameron had thought.

Smith looked at Cameron and Agent McNeil, obviously happy to show off a bit. "Gentlemen, my panic room. Although, I rarely panic so I haven't had much use for it in that sense." Chuckling, Smith walked into the room. "It's fabulous, isn't it? And here is the Ghost Shell drive for which Ms. Reardon is determined to try to cheat me out of two million dollars." Smith reached over and pulled an external hard drive from one of the shelves. It was black, not too big. So benign-looking.

Cameron knew instantly what he had to do; he wouldn't get another chance like this. He could grab Ghost Shell and get Sophia out. It meant not being able to arrest Smith, but it was a trade-off Cameron was willing to make.

Cameron pulled his weapon out and pointed it at Agent McNeil. He knew that man was armed. Smith he wasn't sure about, but knew not to take him lightly.

"Sorry, Mr. Smith. But I'm going to have to take Ghost Shell off your hands." Cam decided to try to keep his undercover identity intact. Let them think he was just stealing from them out of greed. Both Smith and McNeil spun to look at Cam. McNeil made a move toward his weapon. "Nope, Agent McNeil. I need you to keep your hands right in front of you where I can see them. You, too, Mr. Smith."

Cameron kept the weapon pointed at McNeil as he walked over and took the man's gun from its holster.

Anger radiated from Smith's cold eyes. "So you did know Sophia?"

"Nope," Cameron told Smith, popping the *P* in the word as he reached over to take the hard drive from his hands. "But let's just say she convinced me of Ghost Shell's true value and that I could make a lot more money selling it on my own."

"Cam," Smith said, obviously trying to get his temper under control. "This isn't what you want to do. DS-13 is not an enemy you want to have. Even if you kill me, others will hunt you down."

Cameron knew Smith was stalling for time. Fin and Rick would be back with Sophia any minute and Cam would lose the advantage. "I think half a billion dollars will buy me pretty ample security." Cameron looked around the panic room. He had no idea what sort of communicative measures it had. He destroyed what he could see: ripping out a landline telephone and all the cords attached to a computer that sat in a corner. Cameron was sure there were other ways to communicate from inside the panic room, but hoped this would give him enough time to get Sophia out of the house.

Cameron stepped backward until he was just inside the door, weapon still pointing at the two men. "You're going to regret this," Smith spat at Cameron.

"Maybe," Cameron responded and then fired his gun at the keypad inside the door, blasting it into little pieces. Hopefully that would keep McNeil and Smith in there at least a little while.

Now the countdown had really started—somebody was bound to have heard the shot. Cameron stepped all the way out of the room and pressed the button that closed the door on the hidden book keypad. Smith's eyes were still shooting daggers at Cam as the door closed with a resounding thud. Cameron wasted no time and ran out of the office, Ghost Shell hard drive firmly in his hand.

He was carefully heading back down the hall toward the bedroom when he heard Sophia screaming his name in terror.

Chapter Fourteen

When Cameron left to go see Smith, Sophia decided to be ready. Ready for exactly what, she wasn't sure. But when he got back, she wanted to be ready.

Her shoulder was bothering her more than she had let on to Cameron, and it was becoming more stiff and difficult to move. Bending down to put on her socks and shoes caused a throbbing in her shoulder, but Sophia ignored the pain as best she could. A tap on the door startled her.

"Yes?" she asked as she walked slowly over to it. Sophia didn't want to open it, although recognized the lock on the door wouldn't keep anyone out if they were determined to get in.

"A breakfast tray for you, Ms. Reardon," a female voice said from the other side of the door. Sophia opened it hesitantly, but saw it was indeed just a woman with a tray in her hands. Moving aside, Sophia allowed the woman to bring in the tray and watched as she set it on the table and left without another word. The woman closed the door with a resounding thud as she left.

Was it just Sophia's imagination, or had the woman seemed hostile and suspicious? Did she know something Sophia didn't? Did everyone know who she and Cameron really were?

Or was it a woman just doing her job who had other tasks

to get back to and didn't want to waste any time? Also a perfectly reasonable explanation.

See? This was why Sophia wasn't meant to do undercover work. Save that for the trained agents. It was too easy to reflect her own paranoia onto others' actions when there was no tangible reason to think they suspected something.

Sophia walked over to the table where the woman had set the tray. She reached down and took a spoonful of the fruit salad. Poison momentarily crossed her mind but Sophia shrugged and kept on eating. At this point either it was poisoned or it wasn't; she wasn't going to worry about it.

A knock at the door again startled Sophia. Had the woman forgotten something?

"Yes?" Sophia asked as she opened the door. But it was Rick leaning in her doorway, not the woman with the tray.

Sophia tried to shut the door again, but Rick easily blocked it. When he took a step toward her, Sophia jerked back. She realized the mistake instantly—backing up allowed Rick to enter the room and shut the door behind him.

She heard him click the lock and knew she was in trouble.

"You've got on quite a bit more clothes than when I saw you last night."

Sophia ignored that. "What are you doing here, Rick? Cam's not here."

Rick's grin was predatory. "Oh, I know. He's in a meeting with Mr. Smith." He took another step toward Sophia and she backed up again, but realized she was getting close to the bed—absolutely the last place she wanted to be near with Rick in the room—so she turned and strode over to the tray with the food.

"Yeah, that's right, he's with Mr. Smith. But he'll be back in just a minute." Sophia prayed the words sounded more confident than she felt. She picked up a grape and popped it in her mouth in what she hoped was complete nonchalance.

Rick smirked. "I don't think so. Mr. Smith had some pretty important stuff to talk to him about."

"Oh, yeah? Like what?" Another grape. Anything that kept Rick on the other side of the room talking.

The gleam that entered Rick's eyes told Sophia she had asked exactly what he wanted her to ask. "This and that. But mostly about you."

Sophia tried not to react.

"What about me?"

"Evidently you haven't been telling the truth about everything, have you?" Rick made a tsking sound. "Mr. Smith has some FBI agent guy who *really* knows about that Ghost software thing and he basically called you a liar." Rick glowed with glee.

Sophia felt paralyzed with indecision. Did Cameron know what was going on? Had Smith already done something to Cameron? Sophia thought about what had happened to Cameron's partner—Smith had had him assassinated. She couldn't bear to think of anything like that happening to Cam so she pushed the thought aside.

Should she run? Try to find Cameron? Rick was strutting closer, that perverse smirk still blanketing his face. Sophia knew one thing: staying in this room with Rick was not a good idea.

"Whatever. This is just a misunderstanding. I'll just go set Mr. Smith straight right now." She headed toward the door, until Rick stepped right in front of her.

"Oh, don't worry, Mr. Smith sent me in here to get you. Looks like you need to be questioned with force and he knows I'm the best man for that job." Rick chuckled darkly, cracking his knuckles. Sophia felt bile pooling in her stomach. "But I thought you and I could have a few minutes in here first. So I could get a taste of what you were teasing me with last night."

Sophia darted to the side to run around Rick but he was too fast. He grabbed her by both arms and threw her toward the bed. Sophia let out a loud moan at the pain in her injured arm, and spun for the door again. But Rick was ready for her.

"Oh, no, you don't." He grabbed her from behind, wrapping both arms around her. His breath was sour at her cheek. Sophia tried to get away but couldn't and knew that Cameron was too far away in Smith's office to hear her scream. Screaming would only bring more of Smith's men in here. "C'mon," Rick said softly. "I'm not asking for anything you haven't already given Cam. What's the big deal?"

"Let. Me. Go." Sophia held herself absolutely still, since the only other option was wiggling all over Rick. "Why would I do anything with you when you basically just told me you were going to torture me for Smith a few seconds ago?"

Rick's grip loosened just a little. Maybe he never considered the fact that him informing her of upcoming torture wouldn't make her want to jump into bed with him. Sophia shuddered. As if she would jump into bed with him for any reason.

"Maybe we can work out some sort of a trade-off," Sophia whispered, turning. "I give you what you want now and you see what you can do to take it easy on me a little later."

Rick considered that then nodded enthusiastically. "Um, yeah, that sounds good." The lie was plain to see in his eyes and Sophia barely refrained from rolling hers.

"Great. We've got a deal." Sophia forced herself to slide her hands up his arms, as if to embrace him. Rick's foul breath hitting her full in the face was almost more than she could stand. Rick slid closer to kiss her, and although she knew she should let it go further than this without running, Sophia could not force herself to kiss him. She took a slight step back and brought her knee up as hard as she could into Rick's groin.

Rick cried out and dropped to his knees, releasing Sophia. She ran toward the door, cursing as the lock slowed her down. Her fingers felt useless as she tried to get the lock to release. It finally did and Sophia frantically pulled the door open, only to have it slam back shut. She turned to find Rick's hulking form looming over her.

"You're going to regret that," he sneered.

Sophia tried to run, but couldn't get around him. His backhand came without warning and the blow threw Sophia to the ground. From the throbbing in her face, Sophia knew she had to get help. Anybody—no matter who a scream brought in. Rick was going to kill her.

She opened her mouth to scream, but Rick moved quicker than she thought him capable. He was on her in a moment with his meaty hand covering her mouth. "Shut up," he growled.

Sophia immediately panicked. The need for air, to get the hand off her face so she could breathe, consumed her. She clawed at his hand, his face, anything she could reach. Vaguely she heard vile curses emanating from Rick, but paid no attention. Her only thought was for air.

Rick's full weight was on her body now, making everything worse. She bucked and twisted sharply, causing Rick's hand to slip off her face for a moment. Sophia screamed as loudly as she could.

"Cam!" The yell reverberated through the room, but she wasn't sure how much farther into the house the sound went.

It was only a moment before Rick hit her again. The

whole world seemed to spin as Sophia fought to hold on to consciousness. Rick wrapped one hand around her throat. "You will shut up or I'll kill you right now." He squeezed to prove his point and Sophia felt everything begin to dim.

Sophia didn't know how to fight someone this much bigger and stronger than she. She clutched at his hand on her throat, but it didn't seem to affect anything. She just tried to drag air into her lungs past the hand intent on keeping that from happening. It seemed to be a losing battle.

And then out of nowhere Rick's body flew off her. Sophia sucked in gulps of precious air, scampering as far away as possible. Her vision cleared and she realized it was Cameron who had tackled Rick and gotten him off her, and was now in the midst of pummeling the other man. Rick had both height and weight on Cam, but Cam had caught him by surprise. And he obviously wasn't interested in showing Rick much mercy.

A sickening crunch brought a howl from Rick before he fell back onto the floor, completely unconscious. Cameron immediately stopped hitting him. He looked over at Sophia. "Are you okay?"

Sophia nodded, still trying to breathe as deeply as possible. Cameron rushed to her side, wincing and gently touching the bruise she was sure was forming on her cheek from where Rick had hit her. "I'm okay. Just…panicked. No permanent damage done."

Cameron reached over and kissed her on her forehead. "Good, because we have to leave. *Right now*," he told her as he helped her up.

"Smith knows about me." She pointed at Rick's unconscious form. "Rick took great delight in letting me know Smith wanted me brought in to be tortured."

Cameron went over to a large dresser that sat against one wall. "Are you okay enough to help me move this?"

Sophia grabbed the other end of the dresser. "Sure, I think. Why?"

She understood a few moments later when they slid the chest directly in front of the door. Getting in that way would be difficult for anybody.

"I've got Ghost Shell. We've got to get the hell out of here."

"How did you get it?"

"I locked Smith and his little FBI friend in his own panic room. But that's not going to hold him for long." Cameron rushed over and grabbed a jacket out of his bag as well as the Omega Sector gadget thing he'd used earlier. He tossed a sweatshirt to Sophia. "Here, you'll need this. Sorry I don't have anything else. I'm not sure how long we'll be outside."

"Can't you just contact Omega and have them pick us up?"

"No. We have to go on our own." He headed over to the sliding glass door that led to the small deck.

"Isn't Omega our quickest route out of here?" Sophia followed him to the door.

"Normally, yes. But Fred McNeil—the FBI agent Smith has on payroll—knew way too much. Made me think we might have a mole inside Omega, too." He turned and looked at Sophia, trailing a finger gently down her cheek. "I can't be sure either way right now. But I won't take a chance with your life."

"So how are we getting out of here?"

Cameron slid the door open and stepped out onto the deck. The brisk fall air was instantly chilling. "We're going to get as far as we can on foot. I'm going to have someone I trust meet us."

"Can't we steal a car here or something?"

Cameron shook his head. "No. I'm sure Smith would be able to track them with GPS. Almost all newer vehicles can be tracked. Plus, it would take way too long to drive out of here. Air is our best option."

Sophia grimaced. "Okay, on foot to the airfield it is, then."

Sophia followed Cameron outside. She was glad the clothes Smith had sent for her this morning had been casual: jeans, a sweater and lace-up flat boots. She imagined if Smith had known she'd be running from him he would've provided her a skirt and heels. Cameron climbed over the deck railing and jumped the few feet down to the ground, then helped as Sophia did the same. He took her hand and led her around the back of the house carefully.

Sophia could hear some sort of commotion at the front of the house. They didn't stop to see what it was. Cameron just took advantage of it and they ran deeper into the woods. Sophia knew it wouldn't be long until Smith's henchmen would be after them. She held on to Cameron's hand and ran as fast as she could.

Chapter Fifteen

Running as fast as they could while not leaving a trail any six-year-old could follow was a delicate balance. They needed to put as much distance as possible between them and the house. Cameron knew by now Smith and McNeil would've gotten out of the panic room and would have every available person looking for them.

The terrain was all downhill—it was difficult to run and hard on the body. Cameron caught Sophia as she tripped over an exposed tree root.

"Sorry," she said through breaths, gulping air.

"You okay? Let's take a rest."

Sophia shook her head. "No. I know we need to keep going. I'll be all right." But her pale features and clammy hands argued differently.

But she was right, they did need to keep going. These early hours were the most important if they were possibly going to have a chance to escape. Cameron gave Sophia a brief nod, but slowed down a bit. He kept hold of her hand as they continued to work their way downhill. It was un-believable how tough Sophia had been the past couple of hours. Cameron knew trained agents who couldn't keep plowing on the way she had. She had every right to com-plain or ask for him to at least slow down, but she hadn't.

It was impressive. Hell, everything about Sophia was impressive. When this was over, when Sophia was safe, Cameron planned to rectify the mistakes he'd made five years ago. He'd walked away from her once, but he wouldn't make that error again.

But first he had to get her to safety. Her breathing became more ragged so Cameron slowed down. They'd been running for well over an hour. He glanced at the sky overhead—it was starting to look ugly. It wouldn't be long before a storm hit. That was both good and bad. Good because it would make it harder for DS-13 to find them. Bad because the temperature was already pretty brisk. Being soaking wet was definitely not going to be comfortable.

"Where are we trying to go?" Sophia asked now that they weren't running at breakneck speed.

"Back down to the runway where we landed."

"Do we have a plane? Did you change your mind about contacting Omega?"

Cameron was torn. "Honestly, I don't know what to do about Omega. There may be a mole, but if there is one, I have no idea who it is."

"So how are we going to get out of here?"

"I'm going to get a message to one of my brothers. He used to be part of Omega, but got out a couple of years ago. He has his own small airplane. Runs a charter business."

"Okay." Sophia sounded relieved. Cameron didn't blame her. Knowing there was an actual plan made the running a little easier, but not much. Cameron looked up at the sky again. Definitely looked worse than it had just a few minutes ago.

"Ready to pick up the speed a little more? We need to get as far as we can before this storm hits."

Sophia just nodded. Cameron took her hand again and began adding speed to their downhill scamper. They ran silently, talking definitely not a possibility when expending this much effort. Cameron was winded himself, so he couldn't imagine how Sophia was feeling. She never complained, but he could hear her breathing become more and more labored.

The rain came at first in a gentle sprinkle and was almost welcome for its cooling effect at the pace they were keeping. But then the skies opened and it really began pouring. They tried to continue but after falling twice, Cameron knew they had to stop. When he looked closer at Sophia he realized they should've stopped much sooner. There was absolutely no color in her face and she was swaying dizzily on her feet.

"Sophia?" Her eyes looked at him without really focusing. "Soph! Are you okay?"

She nodded but obviously wasn't really hearing anything he was saying. Cameron took a step closer to her. "Soph? Hey, can you hear me?" He said it loud enough to be heard through the pouring rain. Sophia just looked at him blankly.

Cameron put his hands on both her cheeks and was shocked at the heat radiating off her. This was definitely more than just the exertion from running. Sophia had a fever—a high one. Cameron wiped her hair from her forehead, where it was dripping water into her eyes.

"It's okay, baby, you don't have to run anymore. Let's find a place where we can have some shelter." Cameron gently led Sophia over to a nearby tree that had fallen. The huge root that had come out of the forest floor provided a slight overhang. It wasn't much, but it would keep Sophia a little bit drier as Cameron looked for something better.

He bundled her as far back into the tree root as he could and knelt down beside her. "Sophia…" Cam spoke slowly, deliberately. "I'm going to find us some better shelter. I'll be right back. I don't want you to move from here. Okay?"

Sophia seemed to understand. She nodded weakly. "Okay."

Cameron didn't waste any time. Getting Sophia somewhere warm and dry, and figuring out what the heck was wrong with her, was the most important thing. It wasn't long before he found what he needed: a small cave. It wasn't big, barely room for two people to sit up in it, but it was dry. Cameron checked it for animals and critters, delighted when he found only a couple of squirrels, which he quickly chased out.

Sophia was exactly where he had left her, propped against the large root. It didn't look as if she had moved at all from the moment he'd left. As a matter of fact, with her eyes closed, lying so still she almost looked…

Cameron rushed over and knelt beside her. "Soph? Honey, are you okay?" When her eyes didn't open immediately he felt for her pulse at her throat. It was there. Although finding her pulse flooded him with relief, its rapid fluttering concerned him. This was more than just exhaustion from running down the mountain.

Cameron pulled her arm around his shoulders and slipped his arm around her waist. He stood, bringing her weight with him. Sophia didn't wake up but a low moan escaped her lips. Cameron cursed under his breath when he realized he had grabbed her injured arm. Jostling her as little as possible, he brought her slight weight up into his arms and carried her to the cave. Feeling the heat radiating from her—she definitely had a fever if he could feel it through her layers of clothing—Cameron moved as fast as he could without putting either of them in danger of falling. The rain continued to blanket them in its cold misery.

Sophia's eyes opened just a bit as he laid her as gently as he could into the small cave opening. "I don't think I can run anymore," she said, her voice barely louder than a whisper.

Cameron brushed her hair back from her face. "You don't have to run anymore, sweetheart. You have a fever, probably from that cut on your shoulder getting infected. We're just going to rest here for a while."

Sophia struggled to sit up. "I'm sorry I'm slowing you down. I just don't feel very good."

Cameron stopped her minimal progress and helped her lay back down, even though rain was still pouring down on him. "Don't try to sit up. I'm going to crawl in behind you and scoot us both back."

Sophia didn't answer and Cameron wondered if she had passed out again. He tossed his small backpack over to the side of the cave, mindful of the Ghost Shell hard drive in the bag. Then he crawled inside, joining Sophia but careful not to jostle her in any way that might cause her pain. The cave was not very large. It was difficult for Cameron to fit himself into the dark area—he couldn't even sit up to his full height. But at least it was dry.

He eased himself behind her then pulled her backward as gently as he could so her back could rest against his chest. She didn't say anything or make any sounds, just slumped hard against him and continued shivering. Cameron caught her forehead with his hand and laid it back so it rested against his shoulder. He felt the heat radiating from where he touched her, although the rest of her body was racked with chills. He tucked his legs more securely around the outside of hers in an effort to share more of their body heat.

Cameron had some ibuprofen in his backpack. He would allow Sophia, and himself, a chance to rest for a little while, then would give her some. It wouldn't fight the infection, but it would lower her fever for a little while. But he didn't have many of the painkillers, so getting some antibiotics into her system as soon as possible was critical.

Holding Sophia snugly against his chest with one arm, Cameron reached over to his backpack with the other. The Ghost Shell hard drive was still safe inside, and he reached for the Omega communication system. Cameron still wasn't sure who he could trust inside Omega, so instead he made a call to his oldest brother, Dylan. He knew Dylan would be loath to get involved with Omega Sector—or any government undercover work whatsoever—after what had happened to him, but his brother would do it anyway if Cameron asked. And Cameron was definitely asking. The fact that Dylan had his own Cessna airplane at his disposal was a huge plus because no cars were getting up this mountain anytime soon.

Cameron's plan was to get Sophia out with Dylan and back to safety. Cameron wouldn't go with them. Instead he would meet the Omega extraction team at dark and go back to headquarters with Ghost Shell. If there was some sort of mole inside Omega, Cameron wasn't taking a chance with Sophia's life. He knew Dylan, or any of his three siblings, could be trusted. That was as far as Cameron was willing to go when it came to Sophia's safety—only the people he absolutely trusted without a doubt.

Cameron punched his security code into the communication unit. It was so much more than a phone, but in this case Cameron was using it for the simplest of calls. He pushed the digits to call his brother Dylan. He picked up after just two rings.

"Branson."

"Dylan, it's Cameron."

"Cam? Hey, little brother. Haven't heard from you in a while."

"I've been working. You know, the usual."

Dylan did know. He had enough background with Omega Sector that Cameron didn't need to explain further. "Are you done with that…project you were working on?" his brother asked.

"No, Dyl, I'm not. As a matter of fact the project became a great deal more complicated over the last few days. I need your help."

"What's going on, Cam?" Cameron could tell he now had Dylan's full attention.

"I came across some information today that suggests that someone within my company might also be…working for a competitor. Problem is, I'm not sure who that person in my company might be or if it is anyone at all."

Dylan paused for a moment and Cameron could tell he was processing what Cam was trying to tell him. "And you're worried for your safety?"

"No," Cameron told Dylan softly, looking at the small woman lying in his arms. "I can handle myself. But someone else has gotten involved and I don't want her to have anything to do with anybody in my company if there's a problem."

"Roger that. What do you need?"

That's what Cameron loved about his family. They had each other's backs, without needing a bunch of details. That didn't mean they wouldn't needle the details out of Cameron later—him asking Dylan to fly out a lady friend was something he was going to get ragged about pretty hard—but right now all Dylan wanted to know was how he could help.

"I'm about to send you some coordinates. It's a small unlit airstrip in northern Virginia. It's smack in the middle of the mountains. You won't believe it's there until you're right on it. I need you to take my friend back to DC and stay with her. That's it."

"Where will you be going? You staying there?"

"No. I'm heading to DC also, but I'll be getting a ride with my company. It's already planned."

"All right. What time?"

"Dusk." Cameron knew Dylan landing his airplane at the unlit airstrip after dark in terrible weather was risky. They'd be cutting it close, but this would be their best chance. "I'll be looking for you around eighteen hundred. And if mountains and oncoming darkness aren't enough of a challenge for you, the weather here is absolute crap. Pouring buckets. Hopefully it will clear out."

"Sounds like a party. Can't wait."

"Dylan, I need you to get some antibiotics. She's got an infected cut and is running a fever. I don't want her to have to go straight to the hospital when a round of antibiotics will do. She's been through a lot."

Dylan didn't ask where he was supposed to get antibiotics without a prescription. But Cameron knew his brother would have them when he arrived. "Anything else?"

"No. And, Dylan, thanks."

"You owe me one for this, bro." Dylan chuckled. "But what's new?"

They disconnected and Cameron sent the coordinates to Dylan.

Sophia was still asleep lying against him, but moaned softly and was obviously uncomfortable. Cameron decided to give her the ibuprofen to help get her fever down, then maybe she could rest a little easier. He got the small tube out of his bag—it wasn't much but hopefully would help her feel more comfortable until Dylan got there with the antibiotics. He grabbed a water bottle, too.

"Here, sweetheart," Cameron whispered as he put the

pills up against Sophia's lips. "Take these. They'll help make you feel better."

"Cam?" Sophia obviously was groggy. "What's going on?"

"This is aspirin, baby. It will help your fever go down and make you feel better."

"Okay." She opened her mouth for first the pills then the water. "Sleepy," she murmured, then almost immediately slumped back against him again. Cameron took a sip of the water himself then recapped the bottle and returned it to his backpack. He zipped it up so it would be ready to go if they had to leave in a hurry.

"That's fine, go back to sleep." Cameron couldn't blame Sophia for wanting sleep. God knew the past few days hadn't held much sleep for her—for both good reasons and bad. A few hours of rest would probably do him some good, too. Cameron felt his eyes grow heavy as he snuggled Sophia more firmly in his arms.

Chapter Sixteen

Cameron awoke suddenly. He held himself perfectly still. Something had definitely disturbed his subconscious. Had Smith's men found them? He reached over and grasped the SIG he had left lying on top of the backpack.

After a few moments he realized it wasn't a noise outside that had woken him, it was Sophia's labored breathing.

"Soph, are you awake?" He felt her forehead with his hand. She seemed much cooler than she had before they had fallen asleep, her fever much lower. But there was something definitely wrong.

"Yes," she said curtly. Cameron could feel tension bowing her body.

"What's wrong? Is it your arm? Are you sick?"

"I…I…" She couldn't seem to get the words out.

"Is it pain?" Cameron wished he had something stronger to give her. He tried to get her to look at him, but she seemed focused on the entrance to the cave, staring at it intently. "Did you hear something? See one of Smith's men?"

Sophia shook her head, but tension fairly radiated from her. She was clutching at his hands and arms, which were wrapped around her, her breath sawing in and out of her chest, the sound loud in the cave, even with the rain. "What is it, Soph? Tell me, please." Cameron didn't know what to do to help her if he couldn't figure out the problem.

"I can't breathe." She finally got the sentence out.

Cameron cursed under his breath. He had completely forgotten about Sophia's claustrophobia. Evidently she had been too sick to notice the small confines of the cave when he'd pulled them in a few hours ago, but now that she was feeling better...

Cameron immediately released her, unwrapping his arms from around her body so she could move if she needed to. She slid away from him, her eyes still focused on the small entrance to the cave.

"Soph, it's okay. C'mon, let's go back outside." There was no point in making her suffer in here even if it was still raining out there.

Sophia nodded tersely and started scooting toward the entrance. Cameron went with her in case she needed any help. They were almost to the small entrance when Cameron heard it. Some of Smith's men talking. Right outside of where he and Sophia were hidden.

If she went out now, it would mean death for both of them.

Cameron knew not to grab Sophia, but he doubted she heard the men talking over her own labored breathing. He scampered around so he was in front of Sophia and they were face-to-face. She immediately began to go around him so she could get to the entrance he blocked.

"Sophia, look at me, sweetheart." She glanced at him for just a second before her eyes darted back to the entrance. Cameron reached out and as gently as he could, careful not to restrain her in any way, put his hands on both her cheeks. "Sophia, Smith's men are right outside. If you go out there now, they're going to kill both of us."

Cameron watched, heartbroken, as Sophia's eyes darted back and forth frantically between him and the cave entrance. But at least she stopped moving toward it.

"That's right, sweetie," Cameron murmured. "Just look at me. Watch me breathing. There's plenty of air in here. Plenty. Can you feel the breeze?"

Sophia nodded hesitantly. Cameron stayed right in front of her, his face only inches from hers. "Breathe with me. In through your nose, out through your mouth."

For long minutes they stayed frozen right there doing just that. Cameron could hear Smith's men still nearby, and kept his SIG ready in his hand in case he needed it. Why were the men concentrating so hard on this area? Why hadn't they moved on? If Cameron hadn't taken the time to camouflage the entrance to the cave, the men probably would've found them already.

But at least Sophia didn't seem about to rush out there and announce their presence any longer.

"I think I'm okay," she whispered.

"You're doing great. You're amazing. Courageous." Cameron trailed his finger down Sophia's cheek.

"Yeah. It's amazing that a grown woman gets freaked out in a place that obviously has plenty of oxygen and almost gets us both killed. So courageous." She turned away, disgusted with herself.

"Hey," he said, grabbing her before she could get far. "Courage isn't about not having fears. It's about how you handle the ones you do have. You were panicked, but you got yourself under control."

Sophia shook her head and refused to look at him. "No, you don't get it. It's taking everything I've got right now not to burst through that entrance. I'm still not sure I'm going to be able to keep myself from doing it."

"Soph, look at me." He didn't think she was going to, but she finally did. "Even if you handle it one second at a time, you're still handling it. That's all anybody can ask."

Cameron could tell she still wasn't convinced. He

cupped her cheeks with his hands again. "I don't care if you can see it or not. You're still amazing." He brought his lips down to hers.

Cameron worried for just a moment that kissing her wasn't a good idea—what if this just compounded her claustrophobia? But the way she kissed him back eliminated those fears quickly.

When they broke apart Sophia's features were a little less pinched. She still constantly glanced over at the entrance, but didn't seem quite so much as if she was going to bolt for it at any moment.

"I wasn't always claustrophobic, you know," Sophia whispered. "Just since the car accident."

"What accident? Did someone hit you? Was it bad?"

Her eyes darted to him briefly. "Yeah, it was pretty bad." Cameron could see tension heightening in her again. He was about to change the subject when she spoke again. "But no, nobody hit me. I was driving alone—too fast—and I was upset. It was raining and I took a curve too hard and went over an embankment."

That was much worse than Cameron had thought. "That sounds pretty awful. How badly were you hurt?"

Sophia didn't say anything for a while then started wiggling around. Cameron realized she was trying to take off her sweatshirt, although he had no idea why. He helped her slip it off. "Thanks," she told him. "Being cold actually helps me to feel like there's more air. Totally a mental thing, but…" She shrugged. "As for injuries…broke my femur, a couple of ribs, pretty heavy concussion."

Cameron's breath whistled out through his teeth. He'd had no idea. They sat in silence for a few moments before she continued. "When my car went over the embankment it rolled over multiple times." Sophia swallowed hard. "It finally stopped when it hit a tree. It completely crushed in the passenger side of the front seat, and I was trapped. Fortunately, another car saw me go over and called 911, but it took them a while to get the emergency vehicles there. I was hard to get to."

Cameron could see Sophia doing a breathing exercise as she told her story—in through her nose, out through her mouth. "I was trapped there about two hours—although believe me when I say it felt much longer. The car had crushed around me, and I was pretty sure I was going to die. I kept hyperventilating and passed out a couple times, which was a blessing, until I woke back up to that enclosed space."

Cameron understood now why she had panicked waking up in the cave—too much like waking up in that car. "I'm so sorry, Soph." He'd come so close to losing her. Cameron had to touch her; he couldn't help himself. He put his arm around and scooted as close to her as possible, relieved when she didn't move away. He put his face against her neck and breathed in her scent.

He'd almost lost her, and he'd never even known.

Sophia leaned in closer to him. "Physical injuries were pretty bad—I was in the hospital for about a week. It was a long recovery, lots of PT. But I found the mental issues, this overwhelming claustrophobia, to be ongoing. I've been seeing a therapist once a week for almost five years. You'd think I'd have made more progress, right?" Sophia smiled ruefully.

Cameron felt as if he had been punched in the gut. She'd been seeing a therapist for *five years*? He thought the accident had happened recently. If she had been in therapy for five years then...

"Soph, when did the accident happen?"

Cameron could feel Sophia's attempt to huddle into herself. Silence, except for the rain and an occasional sound from one of Smith's men, surrounded them. Cameron

thought maybe she wasn't going to answer—which was
an answer in and of itself.

"The day after you left," she finally whispered.

Cameron struggled to keep himself under control. He
wanted to punch the nearest wall or howl in some primi-
tive rage. It wasn't hard to put two and two together. Sophia
had been upset because he had left and then she had been
in a life-threatening accident. Cameron moved away from
Sophia, trying to process it all and his obvious blame in it.
Cameron couldn't seem to figure out how to form words.
What could he say anyway?

"Soph, I'm so sorry. How can you not hate me?"

Sophia reached over and grabbed his hand. "It wasn't
your fault, Cam. Just a really poor set of circumstances—
bad weather, bad emotional state, bad road to be driving
on. Bad luck all the way around."

Cameron shook his head. Maybe Sophia had come to
that point, but he couldn't—not yet anyway. He thought of
after the accident; Sophia had no family, no one to help take
care of her. And he hadn't been around, had actually made
sure he was completely unreachable, when she needed him
most. Had she tried to contact him? Even if she had wanted
to, he had left her no information whatsoever.

"Soph, I'm so sorry," he repeated. Although how could
words ever make up for what had happened? He couldn't
believe Sophia was willing to even sit here holding his
hand. Willing to be with him in any shape or fashion after
what had happened.

Sophia turned more fully toward him. Cameron found
he couldn't quite meet her eyes. "Cameron Branson, look
at me," she told him and he did, reluctantly. There was no
trace of claustrophobic panic in her features now. Just gritty
determination. "What happened, happened. The accident
was not your fault."

"But—" Cameron began. Sophia put her hand over his mouth.

"No 'buts,'" she said, and, miracle of all miracles, actually smiled. "I'll admit, I was mad for a while—at you, at circumstances, at life in general. But I became stronger because of it all." She gestured around the cave. "And yeah, I still struggle with claustrophobia, probably always will. But I'm learning how to work through each situation one at a time. It's like someone once told me, 'Courage isn't about not having fears. It's about how you handle the ones you do have.'"

Even with Sophia parroting his words back to him, Cameron was going to need more time to process all this. And they were definitely going to need to talk about it more. Sophia had had five years to come to peace with it, but it was a new and gut-wrenching blow to Cameron. But one thing was becoming more and more clear to him: when this op was complete, things were definitely not going to be over between he and Sophia. He wasn't sure he was ever going to have the strength to walk away from her again.

He just prayed, after everything that had happened, he could talk her into allowing him into her life permanently. Because he didn't think he could live without her.

He looked at Sophia more closely. Her face had lost the tension. Her breaths were slow and easy. "You seem to be doing okay right now."

"It's like my therapist says—sometimes it's just about refocusing. In the middle of a panic attack that can be difficult to do." She shrugged and smiled. "But I'm learning."

Cameron couldn't help it. He reached over and kissed her again. He didn't care about Smith's men outside or the rain or their dire situation. He just had to have Sophia in his arms right damn now. When they broke apart they were both breathing hard.

"Now, that's what I call refocusing." Her eyes all but sparkled. "I'll have to remember this next time I'm having issues."

Cameron pulled Sophia closer to him, loving the way she snuggled into his side. Her breathing was calm and even now. They both watched the entrance of the cave, but not with any panic.

Every once in a while they could hear one of Smith's men talking. Cameron grimaced. They were still around here. Why? Passing through in an effort to search for them—sure. But they seemed to be spending more time here than would be expected. And yet they couldn't actually seem to find him and Sophia.

"Why are they still here?" Sophia evidently had the same thoughts as Cameron.

"I don't know. Maybe we left more of a trail than I thought." Cameron shrugged, trying to figure it out. "I covered the entrance pretty well, so unless they get right up to the overhang, they won't see it. I hope." He made sure his SIG was right beside him. It wouldn't do them a whole lot of good, especially if they weren't trying to take him and Sophia in alive, but it was better than nothing.

"Maybe they'll start looking for us somewhere else soon."

Cameron nodded. "I hope so. Getting to the landing strip in this weather will be hard enough without having Smith's men standing right on top of us."

"How long before we need to leave?"

"Pretty soon. It's going to take us at least another couple of hours to get to the landing strip. My brother Dylan is coming with his plane to get you. I talked to him while you were asleep."

"Where is he taking us?"

"He's going to take you back to DC. But I'm not going with you. I have to get Ghost Shell to Omega Sector HQ."

"Oh." Sophia's voice was small. "I guess that will be it, then."

"You mean for us?"

Cameron could barely make out Sophia's slight nod in the dimness of the cave. But he could definitely feel her easing away from him. He reached his arm around her and snatched her back to his side.

"As soon as I get Ghost Shell settled and am debriefed you can expect me to show up at your doorstep. Don't doubt that."

There was silence for long moments. "I want that, too, Cam, so much." A huge *but* hung in the air between them. Sophia definitely had more to say and Cameron was pretty sure he didn't want to hear it. Finally it came. "But I'm not sure our worlds blend. I'm not sure that we're right for each other."

Cameron had been right. He definitely didn't want to hear this. Panic began to bubble up within him. "Soph…" He turned to her so he could look her in the eyes. "I know I hurt you before. I left and then the accident… I can never make up for not being there for you."

"But that's not really it, Cam." Sophia made eye contact, then looked away. "I don't expect you to make up for the past. The accident wasn't your fault and even leaving wasn't something you did to deliberately hurt me. The past is done, and we both have to move on. I'm talking about *now*."

"Sophia…"

"Your world is dark," she continued without letting him speak. "Your life—what you've chosen to do as an under-cover agent—is so important and admirable. But it scares me, Cam." She gestured around the cave. "All of this scares the hell out of me. The girlfriend of an undercover agent needs to be braver than me, more capable than me."

There were so many things Cameron wanted to say in response to that, he hardly knew where to begin. He barely refrained from rolling his eyes. "Are you kidding me? Sophia, you have been thrown into a situation here that is impossible. And without any training you've stepped up and done as well or better than many agents I've known."

He grasped her chin to force her to look at him. "So I don't want to hear you talking any more junk like that. There is not one instance in this entire situation that I've regretted your actions. Except for maybe when you came back for me that first night. That was stupid. But so, so brave." He punctuated the sentence with light kisses on her lips. "And besides, I'm not asking you to become my undercover partner. I just want to be with you."

Sophia gave him the sweetest, softest smile. Cameron could feel his heart squeezing in his chest. *That* smile. That was the one he wanted to wake up to every day for the rest of his life.

His own thought startled him. But then he realized the thought was exactly right: he didn't want to spend another day without Sophia.

"What?" she asked. "Did you hear something? You got a panicked look for a second."

Cameron smiled and kissed Sophia again. "Nope, no panic. Just reality shifting to the way it should be."

"I don't understand." Confusion was clear in Sophia's green eyes as she gazed up at him.

"I know." He smiled. "Just don't kick me out when I show up on your doorstep in a couple of days, okay?"

"Deal." Sophia sighed and snuggled in toward him a bit. "Can we rest for a little longer? I'm still pretty tired for some reason."

"For some reason?" Cameron reached over and smoothed a lock of hair on her forehead. "Your body has been battling through life-or-death situations for the past three days. You've hardly had any rest." He grinned down at her. "Part of that is my fault, I'll admit. Plus you have some sort of infection. How are you feeling?"

"Better. Much better than when we were running."

"Yeah, you were running a fever. The ibuprofen brought it down." Cameron got the remaining pills out of the bag. "Here, take these. We're going to have to head out in just a little bit, in order to meet my brother on time."

"Okay. My arm is pretty stiff. I don't think I'm going to be able to run very fast."

Stiffness wasn't good; it meant the infection was more pronounced than Cameron had thought. "It's okay. We'll make it. Dylan is bringing a dose of antibiotics so we can get that into you as soon as you're on the plane."

"I wish you were coming with us."

"Me, too. But it's better this way."

Cameron prayed he was telling the truth.

Chapter Seventeen

Everything in Sophia's body hurt, but her heart felt light. They were about to make it out of this nightmare. She wasn't in Smith's clutches anymore. She didn't have to make up lies and pray they were the right ones and wouldn't cost her and Cameron their lives. And, come tomorrow, she wouldn't have to wear the clothes that creep picked out for her. For some reason that weirded her out most of all and she wanted out of these clothes Smith had chosen for her as soon as possible.

And speaking of being out of her clothes… Cameron. Sophia felt a little like a giggly schoolgirl. *Cameron Branson* wanted to go steady with her. He was so dreamy. A little chuckle slid out from where she was perched against Cam, trying to rest.

"What?" he asked. She heard the amusement in his voice.

"Nothing." There was no way in hell she was telling him her thoughts.

Sophia had never been able to forget Cameron. She didn't dwell on the past, but he had never been far from her thoughts. She had always imagined they would meet again, but definitely not under these conditions. This entire situation was surreal.

But Cameron wanted them to spend time together when

everything wasn't crazy. Sophia thought back to all those talks they'd had together at the diner before he had joined Omega Sector. Those times together hadn't been sexual—although there had certainly been a sexual undercurrent—but they had been special. Important. She looked forward to having times like that again.

And knowing Cameron wanted them also made it all even more special.

Sophia could've gladly stayed in the cave all day under different circumstances, listening to the rain, snuggling up against Cameron. Her therapist had definitely been right about the refocusing exercises because nothing about the enclosed nature of the cave was bothering her now.

It seemed like just a moment later when Cameron nudged her. "Are you ready to go?"

Sophia nodded and began to put the sweatshirt back on. It was still wet and not very comfortable, but at least it would provide a layer of protection against the rain. "Yep. Are they still out there?"

"I haven't heard anything for a while, but that doesn't necessarily mean they're gone. We're going to have to be as quiet as possible."

They made their way to the edge of the overhang. Cameron gently moved the branches he had used to camouflage the entrance. Motioning her to stay where she was, he headed out of the cave, gun in hand.

Sophia waited, mentally preparing herself to run if needed. Cameron came back a few minutes later.

"I didn't see them. Hopefully they're gone. But try to stay right behind me and be as quiet as possible just in case."

Sophia nodded and made her way out of the cave. The rain still came down in a steady drizzle. She followed along behind Cameron as silently as she was able, but every step they made seemed terribly loud to her.

"We've got about four miles to go and just a little over an hour's time to get there," Cameron told her a few minutes later. "We'll need to pick up the pace. If those guys are anywhere around the airstrip when my brother is landing, he'll be a sitting duck."

"Is Omega Sector coming to the airstrip, also?"

"No, they'll get me out via helicopter. There's a number of places they can do that. I'll establish a place with them soon."

They began a light jog, much less quickly than their run earlier, but it didn't take long for every step to cause a jarring pain in Sophia's arm. And the rain didn't help; it just made her totally miserable. She grimaced but didn't say anything to Cameron. What could he do? She'd have to gut it out until she got on the plane. She could do that.

Thirty minutes later keeping that promise to herself was becoming more difficult, but still she tried. She was relieved when he called for them to slow back down to a walk.

"Hey, you okay?" Concern was written all over Cameron's face. He walked over to her and rubbed his hands gently up and down her arms. Sophia leaned forward until the top of her head rested against his chest. She just needed a break. Just a couple of minutes.

"I'm okay. It's just…" Sophia trailed off. She didn't have to say it.

"I know, sweetheart. You're doing great." Sophia all but snorted from against his chest. "Seriously. It's less than two miles. Let's keep going at a walk."

Walking she could do. More than that? She just didn't know.

"Okay."

Cameron slid Sophia's hand through the crook of his elbow and they began again. He kept his other hand around hers. She must really look like hell if he was keeping this close to her. It definitely wasn't the most stealthy way to travel. She knew he was afraid she would fall flat on her face again.

Sophia could admit she was afraid of the same thing.

Cameron let Sophia set the pace and she moved as quickly as she could. Every step was agony.

They both heard it at the same time. A small propeller plane. Circling not far overhead.

"That's Dylan. Damn it."

"How far are we from the landing strip?"

"Less than a mile. But if any of Smith's goons are in the area, they're going to hear him, too."

Sophia took a deep breath. "Let's move faster. I'll be okay."

Cameron reached over and kissed her hard and quickly. His hands framed her face. "You are amazing."

Sophia tried to smile, but couldn't quite succeed. "Tell me something I don't know. Now quit flirting and let's go."

Cameron took Sophia's uninjured arm and wrapped it around his shoulders. He put his other arm around her waist, anchoring her to his side. He took off at a brisk run, not nearly as fast as he could go, Sophia was sure, but fast enough to take her breath away. She focused all her energy into putting one foot in front on the other and not slowing Cameron down. She'd never forgive herself if something happened to Cameron's brother because of her.

Sophia wasn't prepared for Cameron's sudden stop a few minutes later before they even got to the landing field. She would've fallen to the ground hard if he hadn't had such a tight hold on her. He wrapped his arms around her and swung them both behind a tree and slid to the ground.

"What's happening?" Sophia asked between breaths.

"I saw one of Smith's goons." He shook his head with a grimace and Sophia knew something beyond just seeing one of the men was troubling him.

"What? Is he blocking our path?"

"No. That's just it. He's heading back toward *us*, not the airfield."

"That's bad."

"Yeah, it's bad. Plus, it doesn't make any sense. If he's that close, he should've heard Dylan's plane, too. I have no idea why he isn't trying to intercept Dylan."

"Maybe he has other orders or something."

"Maybe." But Cameron shook his head again.

"Can we go around him?"

"We'll have to. Stay close behind me. But we have to move fast. If the other men know Dylan is here, they'll be headed toward him."

They moved as fast as they could and were both careful to be silent. Sophia could tell when Cameron would spot the man, flinging them both to the ground or behind some sort of forest cover. With every bounce her arm throbbed.

Backing around one of the trees, Cameron cursed under his breath. "We can't catch a break. It's like he knows where we are."

"Could he be tracking us?" Sophia didn't know what sort of equipment DS-13 had, but the ability to track them seemed feasible.

"I thought of that, but if so, they should've found us at the cave. I don't know."

Cameron reached into his backpack and pulled out the communication unit thingy. He punched in digits while dragging himself and Sophia lower onto the ground.

"You landed?" he asked without greeting.

Sophia couldn't hear what was being said on the other end.

"Good. Anybody around?"

More talk from the other end.

"New plan. We've got a tail I can't shake. I'm going to get her to the end of the field and let her run to you. I'll lead whoever's attention I can get off in the other direction."

Sophia caught the word *stupid* from Cameron's brother.

"Yeah, I know. Just get her out. I'll take care of myself."

Cameron hit a button and threw the phone back into his bag. "Are you ready? We're going to make a run for it."

"Um, I was right here. Don't you mean *I'm* going to make a run for it and you're going to get yourself killed?"

"Soph, I'll be fine."

Sophia shook her head. "Didn't I just hear your brother call this plan stupid?"

Cameron grinned and winked at her. "Actually, he was calling me stupid in general, not the plan. We've got to go, baby."

"There has to be another way." Sophia would not allow Cameron to sacrifice himself for her.

"Sophia, listen. I promise I will be fine. Once I get you on the plane, I will be a ninja—fast, silent, stealthy. They won't catch me."

Sophia knew she was slowing him down. If he had to fight or make a real run for it, he'd be much better off without having her to worry about. But she still didn't like it.

"Promise?" His face was right next to hers and she took the opportunity to kiss him briefly.

"Absolutely. Ninja pinkie-swear."

She would've chuckled if she wasn't so scared. "Okay, let's go."

He led her the rest of the way to the airfield as quickly

as possible, continuing the darting between trees and zig-zagging. Sophia only once caught a glimpse of the man who was following them, but he was very definitely only a couple hundred yards away.

Sophia saw the small airplane at the end of the runway. Cameron's brother had obviously tried to make the plane as inconspicuous as he could, but that was nearly impossible.

"Okay, you need to make your way down the tree line to the end of the runway. Don't cut over to the plane until you have as much of a direct route as possible. Use the tree cover to your advantage. Do what we've been doing—darting back and forth between trees."

Sophia's head nodded like a bobblehead doll. "Okay. What will you be doing?"

"I'll make sure I have our tail's attention and head the other way."

"I still don't like this plan."

"You'll be fine."

"It's not me I'm worried about!" Sophia barely remembered to keep her voice to a whisper. "I'm the one about to get on a safe, dry plane."

"I'll be fine. Ninja, remember? I'll be catching a ride with Omega in just a few minutes and will see you in a couple of days." Something caught Cameron's attention in the distance. "But I need you to go *now*. And I need you to keep going no matter what you think you hear or see."

Now Sophia was really scared. But she had to trust that Cameron knew what he was doing. Her head nodded again, but she couldn't force any words through her clogged throat. Cameron took her gently by the shoulders and turned her around then gave her a gentle push toward the plane. Sophia began to run as fast as she could. She pushed past the agony in her arm and the weariness. She knew that the faster she made it to that plane, the sooner Cameron would start thinking about himself and get safely picked up by Omega Sector.

Sophia darted from tree to tree as Cameron had told her. She never saw anyone, but didn't let that change her plan. When she got to the point that the plane was directly perpendicular from her she dashed out of the trees. She wasn't out of the tree line for five seconds before the propellers on the plane started. But not before she heard the *pop* of gunfire. Sophia wanted to stop and look, but didn't. Had Cameron fired or had he been fired at? Sophia had no idea. She ran faster.

The door that became stairs to the plane was lowered and waiting for Sophia. By the time she got there—gasping for air—a man looking remarkably like Cameron, but a little older, was standing at the top. He helped her as she made her way up the stairs and onto the plane. Quickly, he secured the door and showed Sophia where to sit—right next to him in the cockpit—which was open to the rest of the small plane.

Immediately he eased the plane forward and they began to gain the speed needed for takeoff. Sophia scanned frantically through the windshield, looking for Cameron, but found nothing. She told herself not seeing him was a good sign—much better than seeing him lying wounded, or worse, on the ground—but it didn't ease her mind. As the plane pulled into the air, Sophia continued to look but never saw him. She told herself she should be thankful that at least the plane was away safely. Cameron had a much better chance on his own. But she couldn't quite make herself agree.

Cameron's brother took a pair of corded headphones and handed them to Sophia. She was so exhausted and in so much pain that she could barely understand his gesture for her to put them on.

"Hi. I'm Dylan, Cameron's older and much more hand-some brother. So you're the gal who has stolen my little brother's heart…"

Chapter Eighteen

Cameron was willing to consider that perhaps this plan was pretty stupid after all. Or at least it seemed that way as a bullet flew past his head and into a tree just beyond him. He dived to the ground and crawled backward so he could return fire if needed.

At least Dylan had gotten Sophia away in the plane. No matter what happened now—honestly, even if he was captured or killed by Smith's men—Cameron wouldn't be sorry. Knowing Sophia was safe made all the difference. Of course he had no intention of getting captured or killed.

Ninja, baby.

He had made sure he was able to be seen as Sophia was making her way to the plane, pretty much making himself an open target as he saw her streak out of the tree line in a dead run. He was just glad Smith's henchmen had taken the bait and gone after him. Until he'd almost gotten shot in the head. Then he hadn't been so glad. As soon as he saw the plane beginning its trip down the runway, Cameron had dashed for the cover of the woods. For a minute Smith's men seemed undecided about what to do, go after Cameron or the plane—which told Cameron that Smith wanted them taken in alive. The men's indecision had given both Cameron and Sophia the chance to get away without injury.

Cameron peeked his head out from where he was taking cover behind a tree for a split second before pulling it back. Sure enough, a moment later the area around him was riddled with bullets. There were definitely two people trying to pin him down, possibly even three. He had a good idea where one of them was and crawled a few feet away to take cover behind a different tree. Then he came around from the opposite side and fired three shots. A howl of pain reassured him that he had hit his target.

One down. But he knew there were at least two more still out there.

It was time to set up the extraction with Omega. He had to get Ghost Shell far away from DS-13 hands. Cam got as low as he could and belly-crawled for hundreds of feet to put more distance between himself and the shooters after him. It felt like old army ranger times. He pulled out his sat-com device, but could not risk the noise of a voice call. An electronic message was less secure, but his only option in this case.

Cameron punched in his identification code and the code to send a message directly to his boss, Dennis Burgamy. The man was a jackass, and he and Cameron—hell, Burgamy and *any* of the Branson family—rarely got along, but he could get things done and that's what Cameron needed right now.

Situation changed. Imminent danger. Request immediate extraction.

Cameron didn't say it would only be him. He'd deal with that after he figured out if there was a mole or not. After a few moments Cameron received his reply.

Affirmative. ETA 17 minutes.

Burgamy provided a location based on the coordinates of Cameron's sat-com's GPS. Not far, but under fire it would take the entire seventeen minutes to get there.

Warning: hostiles present. May be coming in under fire.

Cameron put the sat-com back in his bag and began crawling forward. It was slow progress, but hopefully it meant he had lost his hunters. Cameron reached the small open area where the helicopter would land just moments before it did. As it lowered to the ground, Cameron could see the agents inside ready to lay down cover fire so he could get in. Cameron took off in a sprint to the helo. It left the ground just seconds after he was on board. No shots came from the woods behind him. Cameron was both relieved and confused.

Cameron sat back on the bench and put on the headset as the helicopter took off. One of the agents who had been standing guard in the doorway of the helicopter with his automatic weapon sat across from him.

"Thought there was going to be two of you."

"Change of plans," Cameron told the Omega agent. "Had to get her out another way."

The man just shrugged. "Thought you said you'd be coming in hot, too." The man looked more upset about that than not having the second person on board.

Cameron didn't know why Smith's men hadn't fired at him. As a matter of fact, he wasn't sure they had even still been following him by the time he had made it to the opening. Cameron hadn't seen anyone since he'd wounded whoever he'd hit before sending the message.

But why would they have stopped following him? That didn't make sense. Had they stopped to help the wounded man? Maybe. Something about all of this was strange. But

Cameron was out, had Ghost Shell in his possession, and although he wouldn't be able to use it with DS-13 again, his cover as Cam Cameron wasn't blown. They thought he was a thief and bastard, but definitely didn't think he was an agent. All in all, not a bad day.

DYLAN BRANSON WAS as charming as his brother Cameron, but in a quieter fashion. He had a silent confidence; definitely not chatty, but not unfriendly, either. They had been in the air for about twenty minutes when Dylan reached back to his bag and pulled out a syringe kit.

"Amoxicillin. A shot in the arm or leg," Dylan said. "Cameron said you needed it for an infected cut. And if you don't mind me saying, you look pretty bad."

Sophia felt pretty bad. The fever was definitely back. She took the syringe and injected it in herself without qualm. An injection was definitely the best way to get the antibiotics into her system quickly.

"There's some aspirin or something in my bag, too. For your pain," Dylan told her. Sophia took three and swallowed them with a bottle of water he found in the bag.

She leaned over to the side of her seat. She was so exhausted. "I'm just going to rest my eyes for a few minutes," Sophia told Dylan. She knew it was rude, but couldn't seem to help herself.

"That's no problem at all," Dylan reassured her. "Rest is probably the best thing for you. It will take us a couple of hours to get there."

He might have said something else, too, but Sophia had no idea what. Her eyes had already drooped shut.

She woke with a start to Dylan's hand gently shaking her elbow. It took her a moment to remember where she was and who she was with, but all in all she felt much better. Or at least less as if she was about to keel over and die any moment.

"Sophia, it's Dylan." He was talking very slowly as if he was dealing with someone with an impairment, which probably wasn't far from the truth. "I've let you sleep as long as you could, but you've got to get up now."

"Are we there already?" It all came rushing back to her. "Did you hear anything from Cameron? Did he make it out?" It was pitch-dark out now. Surely Omega Sector would've already gotten Cameron out by now.

Dylan smiled. "Yes, I got a message from Omega. Cameron made it out, no problem."

Sophia sagged with relief. He had made it. She knew he had promised he would, but when she had heard that shot as she had run to the plane... Thank God Cameron was safe.

"Do you work for Omega, too?" she asked Dylan.

It was like watching a machine turn all the way off, the way Dylan's features completely closed down. "I used to. Not anymore." This topic was obviously not open for conversation.

Sophia was desperate to change the subject. "How long have I been asleep?"

Dylan chuckled and his features relaxed. "Well, the entire two-hour flight, plus landing, plus a couple hours while I did my postflight checklist, talked to a few buddies who work here and even supervised the refueling for my flight tomorrow."

She'd slept through all that? Holy cow. "Sorry." Sophia felt her cheeks burning.

"Think nothing of it. You needed the sleep. If I had any other business to do here, I'd do it. But this is a tiny county airport and there's not much happening around here after dark. And I didn't think you'd like to wake up and find yourself in some strange plane and hangar with nobody around for miles, or believe me, I would've let you sleep as long as you liked."

"Uh, no, I probably wouldn't. Good thinking on your part. I'd like to get back to my own bed."

"I've got my truck around the back of the main hangar. Let's get you home."

Dylan helped Sophia out of the plane and they walked toward the main hangar. As Dylan had told her, there was no one else around, just the two of them. Which, when Sophia caught the reflection of herself in a window and saw how horrible she looked—as she had run down a mountain in the rain and slept in a cave—was probably for the best. She'd hate for anyone else to see her like this.

They stopped to grab a soda and some crackers out of the vending machine in the hangar, all her traumatized stomach could handle. Dylan excused himself to go check on something about his flight tomorrow in one of the small offices and Sophia sat down at the table to consume her meal.

The door at the back of the hangar opened and closed quietly a few moments later. Sophia looked over in the direction of the door but couldn't see anything in the darkness.

"Hello?" she called out. Had Dylan gone over that way and she hadn't realized it?

Nobody responded. But Sophia sensed someone else in the hangar with her. Someone who worked there?

Sophia stood up. She'd go to the office and find Dylan. If this turned out to be nothing then they could just laugh about her traumatized nerves.

"No need for you to get up on our account, Ms. Reardon."

Oh, hell, it was Smith.

Sophia ran. Maybe they didn't know Dylan was in the

office and she could lead them away. She bolted for the door, but one of Smith's men—Rick—caught her. He threw her against the door hard.

"Now, Sophia, why are you running?" Smith was grinning wickedly as he walked toward her. She could see Fin and Marco with him. Marco was wearing some sort of sling on his arm. "I thought we were friends."

"How did you find me?"

Smith's laughter was far from reassuring. "Now, that happens to be a funny story."

Smith walked all the way up to Sophia until he was standing just inches from her. Sophia tried to back up but Rick was right behind her. Smith reached up and touched her neck. Sophia flinched and tried to move to the side, but Rick wouldn't let her. Smith's hand continued its trail to the side of her neck, then her nape, then finally reaching down inside her shirt's collar. Sophia shuddered at Smith's touch, struggling to keep down the crackers she had just eaten. Smith flipped up her collar. He brought his hand back out and held it in front of her face.

Some sort of tracking device. Damn it.

"So this—" Smith waved the tracker right in front of her "—was supposed to keep me apprised of everywhere you went. After I had a visit from a very trusted source who assured me that everything you were telling me about Ghost Shell was untrue, I decided I better keep close tabs on you. And since I was providing your clothes, this seemed like the easiest way, yes?"

Sophia tried to shy away from Smith again, but he moved closer.

"But, and here's the funny part, it seems that when it gets wet, this little tracking device doesn't work correctly. Quite the defect. So when you were running all over the mountain in the rain, this thing would provide only intermittent, imprecise signals. Not terribly useful. And very frustrating for poor Marco here, who got shot by your boyfriend in the midst of this fracas."

Better Marco than Cameron. But Sophia kept her thoughts to herself.

Smith continued with a flourish, "Once you were on the plane and your clothes eventually dried, the tracking device began working perfectly again. So here we are."

Sophia racked her brain for a way out of this. She wanted to protect Dylan, who she knew would be reappearing any moment. But she also knew what Smith wanted: Ghost Shell. And she didn't have it. And honestly couldn't even tell Smith where it was, even if she wanted to. It was at Omega headquarters and she had no idea where that was.

Sophia didn't see any way that she was getting out of this alive, but she didn't see why she would need to take the brother of the man she loved down with her.

"Well, I guess you found me. Congratulations."

Smith finally backed away from her the slightest bit. "Let's just make this easy for all of us, my dear. All I want is Ghost Shell. No need for drama."

Sophia rolled her eyes, not even trying to hide it. She had no doubt whether she gave Ghost Shell over to Smith or not, he was still going to have her killed. "Unfortunately, there's going to have to be a little drama, Smith. I don't have Ghost Shell. Cam does. And I have no idea where he is."

Sophia didn't see the blow coming, but Smith's slap nearly knocked her to the ground. She could taste blood where her teeth cut against her cheek.

"I really don't have time to play games, Sophia. I believe you when you say Cam has Ghost Shell. What I don't believe is that you don't know where he is."

"I'm sorry, but that's true. It seems that the bastard has double-crossed both of us. We split up to get away from you, but were supposed to meet here hours ago. Why else do you think I'd still be here at this tiny little airport?"

She could see that gave Smith pause. But then he shook his head. "I think not. I saw the way Cam looked at you at the party. There is no way he abandoned you. Not even for all the money he could make doing so."

She looked over to see Fin nodding in agreement. Damn. She needed to think of a way to steer them out of the building before Dylan returned.

But she was too late. Dylan stepped out of the shadows. She could see his training—so similar to Cameron's—as he took out Fin with two short punches and an elbow to the chin. Fin dropped to the ground before Smith or his men could even figure out what was happening. Dylan had Fin's gun in his hand and was pointing it at Smith in the blink of an eye.

Marco and Rick both drew their weapons and pointed them at Dylan. But Smith only laughed. He pulled out his own gun, but instead of pointing it at Dylan, he stepped behind Sophia and pointed the gun directly at her temple.

"Oh, just look at this." Smith laughed gleefully. "You just have to be Cam's brother. You two look exactly the same. Exactly the same."

"Yeah, that's right, he's my brother. Why don't we all just put our guns down. Everyone can walk out of here without any injury." Dylan nudged Fin with his toe. "Except maybe this guy here."

"I don't think so." Smith grabbed Sophia's arm to hold her more closely in front of him. The movement jarred her shoulder and she let out a moan before she could help herself. "Oh, I'm sorry, my dear. Is that the hurt shoulder Fin told me about?" Smith turned to look at Dylan. "I'm going to need you to put your gun down." Smith grabbed Sophia's shoulder and dug into it with his fingers. Her screams echoed through the whole hangar. She struggled not to lose consciousness.

"Okay, stop," Dylan told Smith. "Here." He laid the gun on the ground and kicked it over to Smith.

"Unfortunately, your brother has something that belongs to me. I need to get that back." Smith motioned to Rick, who walked over to stand in front of Dylan. At this point Fin was dragging himself off the ground, too. "Bring him outside."

Sophia saw Rick hit Dylan in the face and then the stomach. As Dylan was doubled over, Fin brought his knee up into his face, knocking him all the way backward. Smith grabbed her arm and began marching her toward the door.

"Please, Mr. Smith." Sophia was crying now. "I swear I don't know where Cam is. I would tell you."

Smith walked Sophia all the way to his car. She watched as Fin and Rick dragged Dylan outside, taking shots at him when they could.

"Oh, I believe you," Smith told Sophia. "But if that's his brother, he knows where Cam is, or at least how to get in touch with him."

Fin and Rick dumped Dylan's nearly unconscious form at Smith's feet. Smith squatted down so he could get closer to Dylan. "Tell your brother he has until midnight tonight to bring Ghost Shell to me at the warehouse from the last weapons buy. He'll know where that is. Tell him we start cutting her into pieces at midnight."

Sophia sucked in her breath as both Rick and Smith chuckled. There was no way Cameron would be able to get Ghost Shell to that warehouse. Even if he decided her life was worth the trade—which he wouldn't—Cameron wouldn't even have Ghost Shell anymore after giving it to Omega. Plus, it looked as if Dylan was barely breathing. How in the world was he supposed to get to Cameron? A whimper escaped Sophia.

Sophia was so worried about Dylan lying bleeding in the parking lot that she barely noticed Smith's slight nod to Rick and didn't pay much attention to Rick when he came and stood right in front of her. She finally looked up at him just as his meaty fist hit her in the jaw.

Sophia felt everything go black around her, as she sank unconscious to the ground.

Chapter Nineteen

"All I'm saying is that it would've been better if you had brought in Ms. Reardon, too, so she could be debriefed," Cameron's boss, Dennis Burgamy, argued. Again. In his whiny, nasally tone.

"She will be, in a couple of days. She has a wound that needs treating, and then I'll bring her in." Cameron wasn't about to say anything regarding the suspected mole at Omega. Not with this many people in the room.

Exhaustion and coffee flowed through Cameron's veins. Since his arrival at Omega Sector hours ago, he'd been talking, reporting, debriefing nonstop. Dennis Burgamy was thrilled to get his grubby paws on Ghost Shell. Cameron knew the man would be on conference calls either tonight or first thing in the morning, if he didn't send out a sector-wide email, somehow taking credit for the whole thing, first. What a kiss-up.

But Cameron's real problem was that he hadn't been able to get in touch with Dylan. He hadn't expected to communicate with him while he was en route, but they should've been on the ground now for a while. Cameron told himself there was no need to panic. Dylan and Sophia hadn't been out of pocket for that long, and a number of things could've caused the lack of check-in. Cameron had been without a good sleep for a long time, and under a constant level of high stress since Sophia had walked into that warehouse a few days ago, not to mention the headache he'd carried around pretty constantly since he'd had her clock him. He needed to take all these parts of the equation into consideration and not just assume the worse.

"We have medics here who can treat wounds, Branson." It was Burgamy again, but damned if Cameron could remember what they were talking about. He stared at his boss blankly. "For Ms. Reardon's wound?" Burgamy continued.

Oh. Cameron willed his exhausted brain to form a pithy response, but nothing. He just sat there staring at his boss.

"Okay, everybody out of the pool. Party's over, kiddies."

It was Sawyer. Oh, thank God. Cameron had never been so thankful to see his charismatic little brother. Sawyer patted Cameron on the shoulder and gave him a friendly wink, then proceeded to herd everyone else out of the debriefing room, including Burgamy. Cameron sat down wearily in the chair behind the table, watching his brother work his magic. Sawyer spoke to everyone jovially, slapping backs and cracking a couple of jokes. People almost always did what Sawyer asked them to do, and with a smile on their faces.

Cameron shrugged as his brother led the last person out, asking the woman about her child by name. Cameron had worked here just as long as Sawyer, but didn't even know the woman had a child, much less the kid's name. Sawyer had a way with people Cameron just didn't have. Hell, hardly anybody had it.

"You're a popular guy," Sawyer said to Cameron as he closed the door behind the woman who had just left.

"No kidding." Cameron leaned his head all the way back in his seat and closed his eyes, stretching his long legs out under the table.

"I just heard you were back or I would've been here sooner. So, mission accomplished?"

Cameron shrugged. "Not the way I had hoped it would go down. Smith and DS-13 are still fully active, which pisses me off to no end after what Smith did to Jason. But yeah, I recovered Ghost Shell, so I guess Burgamy considers that a win."

"And this girl I keep hearing about?" Sawyer came to sit down on the other side of the desk. If there was one thing Cameron could count on it was that Sawyer would definitely be interested if a woman was involved.

"Sophia Reardon." Cameron peeked out at Sawyer through one eye.

"*The* Sophia Reardon? The one you have categorically refused to talk about for the last five years?"

Cameron closed his eyes again. "Shut up, Sawyer."

Sawyer chuckled. "So where is she?"

Cameron opened his eyes and sat up straighter in the chair. "She's with Dylan. I had him come get her and fly her out separately." Now he had Sawyer's full attention. "I didn't mention this in the debriefing, but I think we have a mole in Omega." Cameron explained the meeting with Agent McNeil and what had put him on guard.

"Holy hell, Cam. If that's true, we've got a really big problem here."

Cameron nodded. A really big problem indeed. "So Dylan's going to take her home and keep an eye on her until I can get there." Cameron looked down at his phone again. Still no message from either Dylan or Sophia. "He should've touched base by now. I don't know what his malfunction is."

The door to the interview room burst open, startling both men. A young man whom Cameron recognized, but whose name he didn't know, was breathing hard, having obviously run from somewhere.

"Um, Agent Branson. You're needed downstairs in the lobby. Like right now," the man huffed out.

"Which one of us? We're both Agent Branson," Sawyer said.

The man hesitated for just a second. "I guess both of you. But he's asking for you, Cameron."

Cameron and Sawyer both stood. "Who's asking for me?"

"I've never met him, sir, but someone said it's your brother." He looked over at Sawyer. "Your other brother, who used to work here. He's down in the lobby and hurt pretty bad..."

Cameron was sprinting out the door at the first mention of his other brother. Sawyer was right behind him.

DYLAN SAT IN a chair surrounded by security personnel. Although *sat* really wasn't the right word. Cameron's heart dropped into the pit of his stomach when he saw the shape his brother was in. One eye was swollen shut, his nose was most definitely broken and Dylan perched in the chair at a peculiar angle with his arm wrapped around his middle. That pose suggested broken, or at least cracked, ribs. And security was surrounding Dylan as if he was some sort of threat.

Cameron scanned the room and noticed immediately that Sophia was nowhere to be seen.

Sawyer uttered a vile curse when he saw Dylan, and his face echoed the shock Cameron knew lay on his own. Someone had worked their oldest brother over in a way Cameron and Sawyer had never seen. And getting the drop on Dylan was damn near impossible.

Both men lowered themselves beside Dylan's chair so he wouldn't have to look up at them.

"You." Cameron turned back to the young man who had come to get them and pointed toward the main entrance. "Medic. Right damn now." He turned to the security workers. "And you two, stand down."

"He came in with no ID asking for you, Agent Branson. We didn't know who he was. He was barely conscious," one of the security guards said.

"He's our brother," Sawyer told them. "You did the right thing. We'll handle it now."

"Dyl, what the hell happened to you?" Cameron gave no more thought to the security team and gave all his attention to his brother. "Where's Sophia?"

"They got her, Cam." Every word was obvious agony for Dylan. "Smith showed up with his goons at the airport and they got her."

Cameron felt the bottom of his very existence fall out from under him. He all but fell into the chair next to his brother. "Is she dead?"

Dylan shook his head gingerly. "No. No, they plan to keep her alive to flush you out."

Cameron let out a huge breath he hadn't even known he was holding. He was almost dizzy with relief. She was alive, at least for now. Cameron planned to do whatever he could to keep it that way. He couldn't lose her now. Not when he had just gotten her back and realized she was the missing piece in his life.

Dylan shifted in the chair and a moan of pain escaped him. "They want you to bring Ghost something." He tried to shrug but failed miserably. "They said to bring it to the warehouse from the last buy or..."

Cameron finished for him. "Or they'll kill Sophia."

Dylan winced. "The main guy said he'd start cutting her into little pieces if you weren't there by midnight."

Midnight? Cameron glanced at his watch. That was only an hour from now. There was no time to get a team together and prepped for the site. He struggled to tamp down the panic building inside him. Panic wouldn't do any good now.

"You do know what he's talking about, don't you? The Ghost thing?"

Cameron made eye contact with Sawyer. Yeah, he knew what it was, but getting it was going to be much more difficult. Especially now that his boss was probably taking selfies with it in his office at this very moment. There was no way Burgamy was going to give Ghost Shell back to Cameron. Not even for Sophia's life.

"Ghost Shell, yeah. I know what it is, bro."

"Cam, you know this is a trap. Whatever it is they want, as soon as they get it, they're going to kill you and her both. There's at least four of them." Dylan's voice was getting weaker. They needed that medic quick. A glance at Sawyer told Cameron he was worried about the same thing.

"They won't kill us if we have anything to say about it. I've got skills you've obviously lost, big brother," Sawyer chimed in.

"Please," Dylan muttered, his eyes drifting closed. "I could take you right now."

"Dylan." Cameron moved closer so his brother was sure to hear him. He had to know the answer to this, although he was afraid to ask. "Had they hurt Sophia?"

Dylan opened one eye. "The last I saw her, the beefy guy clocked her and they threw her in the trunk. But no permanent damage."

Two medics came barreling through the lobby. Cameron stepped back so they could do their job. After just a few moments they announced that Dylan needed to be taken to the emergency room immediately.

"Hell no," Dylan muttered. "If you two morons are going after DS-13, I'm coming with you."

"You're not going anywhere." The medic turned to Cameron. "We're looking at probable internal bleeding and a collapsed lung. The hospital is not optional," she told him.

"Sorry, bro, you'll have to listen to the pretty doc," Sawyer told him. "No more partying for you today. Although for the first time I wish I could trade places with you." Cameron rolled his eyes as Sawyer gave the medic his megawatt grin.

Cameron leaned in to Dylan one last time. "We'll handle this, bro. You've done enough. We'll see you soon after we get Sophia."

Dylan nodded weakly. Cameron stood up and grabbed Sawyer by the arm. "Let's go talk to Burgamy." After a few steps Cameron turned back to Dylan. "Thank you, Dylan."

But his brother was unconscious.

Sawyer and Cameron jogged to the elevator and pressed the button for the floor Burgamy's office was on.

"You know Burgamy's not going to give up Ghost Shell," Sawyer told him.

"Yeah, I know." Cameron rubbed the back of his neck.

"How well does DS-13 know Ghost Shell? Could we pull off a fake?"

"I don't think so. Maybe with enough time, but not by midnight. They're going to want to test it before making any sort of trade. At least that's what I would do. And they've got a pretty high-ranking FBI agent on the take. If he's there, we definitely can't fool him." The elevator door opened and they began walking down the hall.

"So we need the real Ghost Shell," Sawyer said.

"Yeah."

"Did I mention Burgamy's going to say no when you ask him for Ghost Shell? Not even to save someone's life."

Cameron ignored his brother. He had no intention of asking Burgamy for anything. His weapon was holstered on his belt. Cameron knew this was going to cost him his career and maybe even cause him to spend time in prison, but he didn't care. He was going to force Burgamy to give him Ghost Shell and then was going to get Sophia. And, by God, he was going to get her out alive.

He'd deal with the consequences later.

Cameron knocked briefly on Burgamy's office door then walked in without waiting for a response. Burgamy had one hip propped against his desk and was talking on his office phone.

The Ghost Shell drive was sitting on the desk right next to him. Thank God.

Burgamy shot them both an annoyed glance. "Let me get back to you tomorrow, Director. I'll be sure to give you the whole story then."

Cameron barely refrained from rolling his eyes. Although, why bother hiding his annoyance with this conceited boss when Cameron was about to have much bigger insubordination issues. He put his hand on his holster.

Burgamy hung up and stood, obviously ready to light into Cameron and Sawyer.

"Hey, Burgamy." Sawyer started walking toward the man before Cameron could do anything. "Did I ever tell you about the time I met this ridiculously hot blonde in an elevator at the San Francisco FBI field office…?"

Cameron watched as his brother got to Burgamy's desk, seemed to trip and "accidentally" coldcocked Burgamy in the jaw. Hard. Burgamy fell to the ground completely unconscious.

"What the hell?" Cameron asked.

"Hey, that was better than whatever you were about to do there, Clint Eastwood." Sawyer gestured to Cameron's hand that still rested on his weapon. "Now grab Ghost Shell and let's go."

Cameron shook his head, still a little in shock at what had just happened. "How did you know?"

"Because, sweet heaven, could you have any more of the 'I'm going to get her out no matter what it costs me' look broadcasted all over your face? Seriously. Why don't you audition for a melodrama or something?" Sawyer rolled his eyes. "Save me from people in love."

Cameron followed Sawyer out the door, grateful for his brother's theatrics. There would still be consequences, but not nearly as bad as with Cameron's initial plan. As they jogged to the stairs it occurred to Cameron that it hadn't even bothered him that Sawyer had said Cameron was in love.

Because he was.

Chapter Twenty

Sophia awoke in a dark place. She immediately closed her eyes again but could feel her heart rate accelerate and her breathing become more shallow. Every muscle in her body tensed. She reached around with her hands, immediately recognizing where she was from the tight fit and continuous movement underneath her body.

She was in the trunk of a car.

Sophia's first response was near panic. She stretched out her legs, her arms, twisting all around, trying to see if anything would give or open. Nothing did.

Sophia fought—hard—to stay in control of her own body and mind. She didn't open her eyes. There was no point really; it was dark anyway. Instead she concentrated on breathing in through her nose and out through her mouth. She fisted and unfisted her hands, trying to give the tension coursing through her body somewhere to go.

Refocus.

Sophia thought of Cameron this afternoon in the cave and how kissing him, just being with him, had helped her get her panic under control. He wasn't here now to help her, but she knew Cameron believed in her strength to handle this.

Sophia continued her breathing exercises while she tried to take stock of the situation. She was in Smith's car. The trunk wasn't that small—Sophia felt her breathing and heart rate hitch again, better not concentrate on that—and the car was still moving.

Sophia scooted herself over so she was all the way to the back of the trunk and put her face up against the metal. It was cold, which felt good on her overheated skin, and she could feel just a hint of air flowing in from outside since the car was moving.

That little bit of air helped her to calm down even more. Remembering that it was fall and night—there was no way she was going to overheat—helped even further. Sophia turned at a diagonal so she could stretch out her legs a little more, thankful for the first time for her short stature.

Although she wasn't feeling calm, Sophia wasn't feeling panicked. As long as she was in this car and it was moving, as uncomfortable as it may be, she was at least out of Smith's clutches. Sophia thought of Dylan and shuddered. When she saw him last he had barely looked alive. Sophia thought about how much her jaw hurt after her run-ins with Rick. She couldn't imagine the shape Dylan was in. Would he even be able to get the message to Cameron?

And how would Cameron be able to get Ghost Shell to trade for her life? No law enforcement agency would be willing to risk something like Ghost Shell falling back into DS-13's hands. Omega Sector would be no exception. Not to save one single person's life. And Sophia couldn't blame them.

She had to face the fact that she might be on her own. Yeah, Cameron would try to help, if Dylan had even been able to get the message to him, but without Ghost Shell there was no way they were walking out of there. But she had to face it, even *with* Ghost Shell there was no way Smith was going to let them walk out of there.

Sophia shifted again to allow her torso to stretch out and

felt something hard up against her hip. She reached back to shift it out of her way. A tire iron.

A tire iron.

She brought it in front of her and clutched it like a baby. It wasn't much, but it was something. She wasn't going down without a fight.

They drove for a long time before the road got rougher and they slowed. They must be getting near the warehouse. Sophia wondered how long it was until midnight. She had no idea how long she'd been in this trunk. Soon the car pulled to a stop. Once again Sophia had to focus on keeping calm. Without the air flowing through the crack she'd found in the trunk, it seemed so much more difficult to breathe. Sophia focused on her breathing. She had to be ready. She'd only have one chance to take them by surprise when they opened the trunk. She couldn't—she *wouldn't*—allow panic to overwhelm her.

THE CLOCK WAS ticking in more ways than one. It was getting close to midnight—Smith's deadline. But it also wouldn't be much longer before his boss figured out what was going on. All Burgamy would have to do is talk to one of the medics who treated Dylan, or the security team who escorted him in, and Burgamy would know where they were headed. Either way they had to get this done, and soon.

He and Sawyer were outmanned and outgunned. Under any other circumstances Cameron would also admit they were walking into a situation where the hostage might already be dead. But he refused to even entertain that notion right now. Sophia was not dead.

He could barely stand the thought of her being trapped in the trunk of a car. After what he saw with her today, in a cave that comparatively was much more open than a trunk, Cameron could only assume Sophia would be paralyzed by fear and panic. His white-knuckled grip on the steering wheel became even tighter.

"So what's the plan?" Sawyer asked him. They were only a few minutes from the warehouse.

"To be honest, man, I don't have a good plan."

"A good plan being where we all make it out alive and DS-13 doesn't end up with Ghost Shell?"

"Yeah. Got any ideas?"

"My good ideas started and ended with clocking Burgamy in the jaw." Sawyer chuckled softly.

"I think our best bet is for me to drop you around back, then you try to get somewhere that is hidden but you can pick off one or two of them," Cameron told him.

"But Dylan said there were at least four of them. You think you're going to be able to take down two or more before they get you?"

Honestly, no. Cameron didn't think that. But what choice did he have? His primary objective was to allow Sophia to make it out alive. Making it out himself would just be a bonus. But Cameron knew they couldn't let Ghost Shell get taken by Smith. They would use it to trade for Sophia's life, but definitely not let DS-13 leave with it.

"Sawyer, no matter what, we can't allow DS-13 to leave with Ghost Shell in its fully functional form. Even though we took it from Omega, I just want you to know that I'm aware of that. It's more important than any of our lives."

Sawyer leaned over and winked at Cameron, grinning. "Don't sweat it, brother. I plan to pop a cap in some DS-13 ass if it comes down to it. That hard drive will not make it out of the warehouse in one piece if DS-13 has it."

Cameron shook his head. Sawyer was crazy, but he understood what was at stake here.

Cameron pulled the car behind the warehouse next door and dropped Sawyer off so he could make the rest of the way on foot. Then he drove slowly to the warehouse where Smith and his men waited. It was five till midnight.

Smith had pulled his vehicle all the way into the warehouse so Cameron did the same. Was Sophia still in that trunk? Had she passed out? Hyperventilated? Was she wounded? Injured as Dylan had been? Cameron pushed those thoughts aside; he couldn't let his concern about Sophia cloud his decision making. He just needed to get her out alive. Anything else she could heal from.

But Cameron did wish he knew what sort of physical condition Sophia was in. Would she be able to run? Would she need to be carried? If he had to stay behind, would she be able to get out on her own? With her having been trapped in the trunk he could only assume the worst.

The only saving grace in this entire situation was that Smith and DS-13 were desperate to get their hands on Ghost Shell in working condition. It would be of no use to them if it was damaged. Ghost Shell would be Cameron's hostage.

He prayed it would be enough.

Smith was standing beside his vehicle. Rick was sitting on the trunk, which was facing Cameron's car, a big grin on his face. Marco, arm in a sling, stood perched beside Rick, leaning against the car. Cameron couldn't see Fin anywhere around. He hoped Sawyer had eyes on him, and anyone else who might be up in the rafters.

Cameron took out his weapon and threw the holster onto the seat next to him. He picked up Ghost Shell and held the drive directly in front of his chest. As he got out of the car he wanted to make sure that everyone in DS-13 knew if they shot him, he was taking Ghost Shell down with him. It was the only protection he had.

"Cam, right on time. How professional of you," Smith announced in a pleasant voice that didn't fool Cameron for a second.

"Well, my brother said you asked so politely."

Smith gave a condescending smile. "I do find violence so distasteful, Cam. But it was so important that we give the right message and your brother was quite useful for that effect." Rick snickered from his perch on top of the trunk, but Cameron kept his attention focused on Smith.

Cameron could feel tension cording his neck and struggled to hang on to his temper. This bastard had killed his partner, had nearly killed his brother and was standing there looking positively gleeful only ten feet in front of him. Cameron was sorely tempted to put a bullet in Smith right here and now, and then let things happen as they may. Only the thought of Sophia getting hurt—or worse—kept him from doing so.

Cameron kept his SIG pointed directly at Ghost Shell. "Let's just make one thing clear from the start. If I go down, this—" Cameron rocked Ghost Shell back and forth with his hand "—gets blown to bits. Remember that. And make sure Fin and whoever else is up there knows it, too, wherever they are."

Smith looked annoyed now. "I'm sure everyone knows how important Ghost Shell is."

Damn. Cameron had hoped Smith would call out to Fin. So much for pinpointing Fin's location. Cameron just hoped Sawyer would find him. And soon.

"Where's Sophia?" Cameron asked.

Now Rick chuckled again and used his weight to make the trunk of the car bounce up and down. "She's in here, Cam. She's probably not real excited about that, do you think?" He banged on the trunk loudly with his fist, obviously enjoying the thought of Sophia's terror. When there was no response from inside, Rick continued, "Nothing. Must have gotten scared and passed out. Poor thing."

Rick didn't even know the half of it since he wasn't

aware of Sophia's claustrophobia. Cameron longed to wipe that sneer off Rick's face.

"Look…" Cam took a few steps closer to them so he wouldn't have to yell. All three men drew their weapons and pointed them at him. "Whoa, everybody simmer down. I just wanted to say that I'm sorry. I obviously made the wrong choice teaming up with Sophia and I got greedy. And I don't expect you to trust me again or do any business with me anymore. All I want is for Sophia and me to get out of here alive."

"Well, you give us Ghost Shell right now and I don't see any reason why you both can't walk out of here," Smith told him. Cameron didn't believe him for a second. "Why don't you go ahead and give us Ghost Shell and then we'll let Ms. Reardon out."

"Um, I don't think so. Why don't you let Sophia out *then* I'll give you Ghost Shell." Cameron hoped Sawyer was in the ready position. Once Rick opened the trunk and Cameron was able to see what condition Sophia was in, he could figure out a plan. She hadn't made any noise from inside the trunk. If she was unconscious or nonfunctional—which was all that could be expected after being locked in a trunk for hours—Cameron wouldn't be able to assist her and keep his gun pointed at Ghost Shell.

At best Cameron was hoping to get Sophia to his car before giving Smith Ghost Shell and the shooting started. At worst… Well, there were a lot of scenarios that fit the "at worst" profile. Especially with three drawn weapons pointing directly at him.

Smith gestured to Rick and he jumped down from the trunk. He turned and unlocked it, pulling it up. Cameron could see Sophia's still form lying there unmoving. Her eyes were closed. He prayed she was just unconscious.

Rick motioned to Marco. "She's passed out. Help me get

her out of here." Marco moved in to help as best he could with one arm in a sling.

Cameron had no warning, but neither did any of the other men. With both Rick and Marco leaning over the trunk to get her out, Sophia came up swinging a tire iron. She hit Marco on the side of the head and he fell instantly to the ground. She hit Rick, too, but only his shoulder. He fell to the side of car, cursing vilely.

Cameron instantly recognized this for what it was: the only chance for success they were going to have. He turned his weapon at Rick and fired two shots into his chest just as the man was pulling his own gun up to shoot Sophia. Cameron dived for the cover of the car as bullets began flying from up in the catwalk of the warehouse. He felt a searing burn in his shoulder, but pushed away the pain. A few moments later Cameron heard a scream and the gun-fire from above stopped. Wherever Fin was, Sawyer had found him. That left only Smith.

"Soph? Are you okay?" She was still in the trunk.

"Yes, I'm all right. I think." Cameron had never been so relieved to hear anyone's voice in his entire life. She sounded freaked out—who could blame her?—but she was alive.

"Can you stay in there for just a little while longer?" Cameron whispered. "Smith is still around here some-where."

Sophia's voice was strained. "Hurry."

Cameron tried to apply pressure to the wound on his shoulder as he got up. He kicked Marco's and Rick's guns away from them as he walked by their motionless forms, just in case. Outside Cameron could see the flashing lights of law enforcement vehicles on their way. Evidently Bur-gamy had figured out where they were. Cameron still had Ghost Shell in his possession.

"Cops are coming, Cam," Smith called out from behind Cameron's car. "Time for both of us to go."

"I don't think so, Smith," Cameron responded. Now that he knew where Smith was, Cameron began to make his way across the warehouse, silently. No more talking from him.

"The only way we get out of this is together, Cam. If we both get caught, I've got connections, but you don't. I'll make sure all this gets pinned on you and Sophia. You don't want Sophia to go to jail, do you, Cam?"

Just keep talking, jerk. Cameron was almost to him.

"Give me Ghost Shell, we'll all get out of here and let bygones be bygones. You can see the lights, Cam. They're almost here. No need for us to get arrested."

Cameron stepped around the end of his car and brought his SIG up against Smith's head, since Smith was still looking the other way, thinking Cameron was with Sophia. Keeping his gun firmly against Smith's skull, he reached over and grabbed the man's weapon out of his hand before he could turn it on Cameron.

"Actually, you're right, Smith. There's no need for *us* to get arrested. Just you. You're under arrest, you son of a bitch, for the murder of a federal agent, kidnapping, assault and a whole slew of things too long to even mention here."

Chapter Twenty-One

"All I'm saying is that watching you come flying out of that trunk, tire iron swinging, was the sexiest thing I've ever seen." Cameron sat in a reclining hospital chair, one arm wrapped around Sophia with her snuggled up against his uninjured side. His other arm was in a sling from the bullet he'd taken at the warehouse, which fortunately hadn't done any permanent damage.

Sophia wanted to get up to make sure she wasn't hurting Cameron or making him feel uncomfortable, but every time she made any sort of movement away from him he would tuck her more thoroughly back to his side.

Not that she wanted to be anywhere else.

"True story," Sawyer called from his seat across the room.

"There's no way you could've seen it from where you were," Cameron scoffed at Sawyer.

"I don't have to have seen it." Sawyer winked at Sophia. "A woman like Sophia, jumping out swinging? Hell yes, that's sexy."

Sophia felt her cheeks burning.

"Don't let them embarrass you, Sophia." That much softer sentence came from Dylan in his hospital bed. He seemed to be out of the woods, but still recovering from the beating he had taken at the hands of Smith's men, two of whom were now dead while two, Smith included, were in custody. Ghost Shell was safely back at Omega Sector, although Sophia understood there was some sort of *incident* where Sawyer had tripped and accidentally punched his boss.

Sophia had been told about the incident earlier today by Juliet, Cameron's sister. She also worked at Omega, although not as a field agent. At least not anymore. She had stopped by earlier to check on her brothers and promised to be back later that day after she tried to smooth things over with their boss for her brothers as best she could.

"So, are you guys going to get fired?" Sophia asked, desperate to turn the topic of the conversation to anything but her and the tire iron.

"Nah." Sawyer's confidence was reassuring. "Like I put in my initial report, I am just such a clumsy bastard. I tripped over my own size twelves and just happened to catch Burgamy in the jaw on the way down. Bad luck all around. Then everything just happened so fast. We were trying to call a medic and Dylan here came stumbling in and we just made a judgment call."

Sophia looked up at Cameron from her nook in his shoulder. "Really?"

Cameron just shrugged.

"Besides," Sawyer continued, "we had it all under control from the beginning at the warehouse. Perfect plan, perfectly executed."

Sophia saw Cameron roll his eyes. Whatever the plan had been, it definitely hadn't been perfect. But she didn't push it any further. She just didn't want Cameron or Sawyer to get in trouble because of her.

"All right, kiddos, I'm out for a few hours if you're going to be staying here for a while, Cam." Sawyer stood up. "I better go help Juliet keep Burgamy from torching my desk. I'll be back in a bit. Try to stay out of trouble while I'm gone."

Cameron nodded. "No problem. Let me know if you need me to come help put out fires."

Sawyer walked over to the chair Cameron and Sophia were lying in. "Sophia…" He held his hand out to her. Sophia tried to get up from Cameron's side, but Cameron wouldn't let her. Sawyer saw it all and chuckled. "No, don't fight him. I'm glad to see Cameron's finally got the good enough sense not to let someone like you go. Better late than never. Welcome to the family." He winked at her then turned and headed out the door.

Sophia was mortified at what Sawyer had said. Would Cameron think Sophia meant that as a clue about where she wanted their relationship to go? "Um, I'm sorry Sawyer said that. I don't know what he meant."

"I do," Cameron told her, head laid back peacefully against the chair, eyes closed.

"You do? Oh, good." Sophia was all but stammering so she stopped talking. But then couldn't help herself. "What? What did he mean?"

Cameron turned so they could look face-to-face at each other. "He meant that I'm in love with you and I'm going to spend however long it takes to make you understand that and convince you to marry me."

"Uh…uh…" Sophia couldn't seem to remember any words in the entire English language.

"It doesn't have to be right now," Cameron continued, smiling at her and stroking her hair away from her face. "We can take as long as we need. As long as you understand that I'm not letting you out of this chair until you say yes."

There was a chuckle from the bed. Sophia had totally forgotten that Dylan was there trying to rest. But she didn't care about Dylan being there, didn't care if the entire hospital could hear them.

"Do you really mean that? You didn't suffer any sort of head injury last night, did you?"

Another chuckle from the bed.

"No." Cameron chuckled a bit, too, but then his laughter faded. "I promise I am of very sound mind. Soph, when I found out Smith had you, it had never been more clear to me that you are the most important thing in my world."

Sophia started to speak, to assure Cameron of the same thing, but he put his finger over her lips to hush her. In his eyes were all the emotions she had always wanted to see. "I've lived without you for five years, and have cursed my own stupidity each day. I don't want to live without you anymore, Sophia."

This was the man she had loved for years, whom she had given up on ever having a future with. Sophia scooted up so she could press her lips to Cameron's. "Then don't."

* * * * *

*Janie Crouch's OMEGA SECTOR series
continues next month with Sawyer's story.
Look for COUNTERMEASURES wherever
Harlequin Intrigue books are sold!*

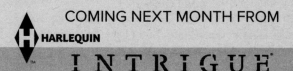

COMING NEXT MONTH FROM

HARLEQUIN

INTRIGUE

Available January 20, 2015

#1545 CONFESSIONS
The Battling McGuire Boys • by Cynthia Eden
Framed for murder, Scarlett Stone is desperate and turns to private investigator—and her former lover—Grant McGuire for help. If Grant is going to keep Scarlett at his side and in his bed, he has to stop the killer on her trail...

#1546 HEART OF A HERO
The Specialists: Heroes Next Door
by Debra Webb & Regan Black
Specialist Will Chase and trail guide Charly Binali race through the Rockies to stop a national security threat. When a single misstep could be their last, Charly must trust her life and her heart to this handsome stranger.

#1547 DISARMING DETECTIVE
The Lawmen • by Elizabeth Heiter
FBI profiler Ella Cortez's hunt for a rapist takes her to the Florida marshes, into the arms of homicide detective Logan Greer, and into the path of a cunning killer. Falling in love could be deadly...or the only way to survive...

#1548 THE CATTLEMAN
West Texas Watchmen • by Angi Morgan
Cattleman Nick Burke and DEA agent Beth Conrad are opposites—but they have to fake an engagement to trap gunrunners on Nick's ranch. Will they overcome their differences to close the case and find a love that is all too real?

#1549 HARD TARGET
The Campbells of Creek Bend • by Barb Han
Border Patrol agent Reed Campbell finds Emily Baker hiding out in a crate of guns smuggled into Texas. He knows keeping her safe will be hard—but keeping his hands to himself might be nearly impossible...

#1550 COUNTERMEASURES
Omega Sector • by Janie Crouch
Omega agent Sawyer Branson was sent to safeguard Dr. Megan Fuller while she neutralized a dangerous weapon that had fallen into enemy hands. Can Sawyer protect her long enough to finish the countermeasure, or will he have to choose between his agency and his heart?

———————

YOU CAN FIND MORE INFORMATION ON UPCOMING HARLEQUIN® TITLES, FREE EXCERPTS AND MORE AT WWW.HARLEQUIN.COM.

HICNM0115

REQUEST YOUR FREE BOOKS!
2 FREE NOVELS PLUS 2 FREE GIFTS!

HARLEQUIN®

INTRIGUE®

BREATHTAKING ROMANTIC SUSPENSE

YES! Please send me 2 FREE Harlequin Intrigue® novels and my 2 FREE gifts (gifts are worth about \$10). After receiving them, if I don't wish to receive any more books, I can return the shipping statement marked "cancel." If I don't cancel, I will receive 6 brand-new novels every month and be billed just \$4.74 per book in the U.S. or \$5.24 per book in Canada. That's a savings of at least 14% off the cover price! It's quite a bargain! Shipping and handling is just 50¢ per book in the U.S. and 75¢ per book in Canada.* I understand that accepting the 2 free books and gifts places me under no obligation to buy anything. I can always return a shipment and cancel at any time. Even if I never buy another book, the two free books and gifts are mine to keep forever.

182/382 HDN F42N

Name _____ (PLEASE PRINT) _____

Address _____ Apt. # _____

City _____ State/Prov. _____ Zip/Postal Code _____

Signature (if under 18, a parent or guardian must sign) _____

Mail to the **Harlequin® Reader Service:**
IN U.S.A.: P.O. Box 1867, Buffalo, NY 14240-1867
IN CANADA: P.O. Box 609, Fort Erie, Ontario L2A 5X3
**Are you a subscriber to Harlequin Intrigue books
and want to receive the larger-print edition?
Call 1-800-873-8635 or visit www.ReaderService.com.**

* Terms and prices subject to change without notice. Prices do not include applicable taxes. Sales tax applicable in N.Y. Canadian residents will be charged applicable taxes. Offer not valid in Quebec. This offer is limited to one order per household. Not valid for current subscribers to Harlequin Intrigue books. All orders subject to credit approval. Credit or debit balances in a customer's account(s) may be offset by any other outstanding balance owed by or to the customer. Please allow 4 to 6 weeks for delivery. Offer available while quantities last.

Your Privacy—The Harlequin® Reader Service is committed to protecting your privacy. Our Privacy Policy is available online at www.ReaderService.com or upon request from the Harlequin Reader Service.

We make a portion of our mailing list available to reputable third parties that offer products we believe may interest you. If you prefer that we not exchange your name with third parties, or if you wish to clarify or modify your communication preferences, please visit us at www.ReaderService.com/consumerschoice or write to us at Harlequin Reader Service Preference Service, P.O. Box 9062, Buffalo, NY 14269. Include your complete name and address.

HI13R

"I need you," she told him as she wet her lips. "I'm desperate, and without your help…I don't know what's going to happen." She glanced over her shoulder, her nervous stare darting to the door.

"Scarlett?" Her fear was palpable, and it made his muscles tense.

"They'll be coming for me soon. I only have a few minutes, and please, *please* stick to your promise. No matter what they say."

He shot away from his desk, his relaxed pose forgotten as he realized that Scarlett wasn't just afraid. She was terrified. "Who's coming?"

"I didn't do it." She rose, too, and dropped her bag into her chair. "It will look like I did, all the evidence says so…but I didn't do it."

He stepped toward her, touched her and felt the jolt slide all the way through him. Ten years…*ten years*…and it was still there. The awareness. The need.

Did she feel it, too?

Focus. "Slow down," Grant told her, trying to keep his voice level and calm. "Just take it easy. You're safe here." *With me.*

But that wasn't exactly true. She was in the most danger when she was with him. Only Scarlett had never realized that fact.

"Say you'll help me," she pleaded. Her tone was desperate. She had a soft voice, one that was perfect for whispering in the dark. A voice that had tempted a boy…and sure as hell made the man he'd become think sinful thoughts.

"I'll help you," Grant heard himself say instantly. So he still had the same problem—he couldn't deny her anything.

Her shoulders sagged in apparent relief. "You've changed." Then her hand rose. Her fingers skimmed over his jaw, rasping against the five o'clock shadow that roughened his face. They were so close right then. And memories collided between them.

When she'd been eighteen, he'd always been so careful with her. He'd had to maintain his control at every moment. But that control had broken one summer night, weeks after her eighteenth birthday…

I can still feel her around me.

"Grant?"

She wasn't eighteen any longer.

And his control—

He heard voices then, coming from the lobby.

"Keep your promise," Scarlett said.

What the hell?

He pulled away from her and walked toward the door.

Those voices were louder now. Because they were…shouting for Scarlett?

"Scarlett Stone…!"

"They were behind me." Her words rushed out. "I knew they were closing in, but I wanted to get to you."

He hated the fear in her voice. "You're safe."

"No, I'm not."

Find out what happens next in
CONFESSIONS
by New York Times *bestselling author*
Cynthia Eden, available February 2015 wherever
Harlequin Intrigue® books and ebooks are sold.

JUST CAN'T GET ENOUGH?

Join our social communities
and talk to us online.

You will have access to the latest
news on upcoming titles and special
promotions, but most importantly,
you can talk to other fans about your
favorite Harlequin reads.

Harlequin.com/Community

Facebook.com/HarlequinBooks

Twitter.com/HarlequinBooks

Pinterest.com/HarlequinBooks

JUST CAN'T GET ENOUGH
ROMANCE
Looking for more?

Harlequin has everything from contemporary, passionate and heartwarming to suspenseful and inspirational stories.

Whatever your mood, we have a romance just for you!

Connect with us to find your next great read, special offers and more.

Facebook.com/HarlequinBooks
Twitter.com/HarlequinBooks
HarlequinBlog.com
Harlequin.com/Newsletters

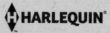

HARLEQUIN®

A *Romance* FOR EVERY MOOD™

www.Harlequin.com